I0668228

KandiTreats

Tanisha Wilson

Copyright © 2012 Tanisha Wilson

All rights reserved.

ISBN:0692246045

ISBN-13: 978-0692246047

Table of Content

Chapter One

Chapter I

It was an attractive Tuesday. The breeze from the ocean seeped through the window screen with a delightful ubiety. I found myself in the company of a beautiful woman.

The girl told me that she was 26 years old, but I knew that she was no older than 18. She lied about her age hoping that the business world would take her seriously.

At first glance she appeared discerning, knowing that every detail of a woman's identity could make or break her. But, a keen eye could see that she was inexperienced.

I stood there smiling, shaking the hand of an imperil girl, who was oblivious that her cognitive dissonance, would lead to her demise.

Her distinguished Mandarin accent and the innocent look in her eyes was all that I was after. She was perfect, men loved chicks like her, and I had been watching her for weeks.

My research gave me insight that she didn't have family nearby and she certainly didn't have many friends. She spent most Sundays alone and hardly ever went out on her days off.

In any case, she owned a business. It was a financially fruitless massage parlor that offered facials, eyebrow and bikini waxing. No matter how unsuccessful, the fact that her ambition drove her to entrepreneurial status was impressive.

I had her under the impression that I was there for a job, but I was after her soul. I turned in my resume a week prior somehow knowing that she would call with no delay.

She scheduled a morning interview at 9:30am. I was there at 9:15am and at 9:20am the catechism began.

She introduced herself as Betty. She was a tiny woman, no taller than 5'4". She was awfully poised, so much so that I held off trying to mirror her body language to impress her.

I interpreted her movements as that of a dishonest woman. It didn't help that she lied about her age. Still, somehow she was sexy enough and flattering.

"I see here from your resume that you don't have any prior experience and you just passed state board. How would you respond to an irate customer who is using foul language?" She asked.

I placed my hands in my lap and responded; "Well, I would be patient, I surely wouldn't curse back at her. Listen, if you give me an opportunity, you will learn that I am smart, energetic and I am great at multitasking."

Although Betty had lived in the states for a few years and was clever enough to start her own business, she still spoke English in incomplete sentences.

"OK Michelle I believe you, and lucky for you I need worker real bad. You work hard, I train you to do thing my way. I am going to give you chance to prove yourself."

Betty thought that she was interviewing me, that I'd be working for her, but in reality, things were quite the opposite—she would be working for me.

I had an ulterior motive. I smiled at her, remained

polite and after speaking with Betty, I guessed that it would take no more than two weeks to turn her small salon into a full service prostitution den.

If Betty was only a little smarter she would have thought of the idea first, because what Betty didn't realize, was that she was married to the game and there was no way out for her.

Anthony, my old mentor from my early days in East Oakland, always would say, "Game is to be sold not told." Besides, I wanted this place for myself.

Betty shook my hand after offering me the job and she told me that I looked young for my age. I smiled and nodded, "So do you."

I asked one last important question, to be sure that she lived alone, "Where is your family?" She smiled back, *"Oh no, no family here, family in Hong Kong; I save money and open my own business. It just me here. I have two employees my other girl- her move- New York City!"*

The girl to which she was referring was my decoy, Cindy. I would send Cindy to investigate local saloons. I needed to ensure that they weren't soliciting tricks and that no outsiders were moving into our territory. Cindy's job was to work for them or befriend the owner for a short period.

Cindy only worked for Betty for one month, before we realized who she was. Once it was verified that Betty was indeed Joy from Kansas City, my goal was to coerce her into our stable as rapidly and cautiously as possible.

Betty and Ramone

Betty was a former slave-hoe from Kansas City, imported directly from Hong Kong. Her birth-given name was Joy. While in her country, Betty went to a casting call for models. Betty was seeking employment to earn extra money; she wanted to help support her family. The modeling agency turned out to be a human trafficking ring. Betty was kidnapped along with 9 other girls. Betty was 12 at the time.

Betty was a strong-willed girl. Her pimp mattressed and raped her 50 times before he was able to break her in. Under usual circumstances, it only took 15 John's to persuade a hoe to comply.

The clientele that Betty's kidnappers catered to

were men of prestige—diplomats, lawyers, and congressmen. They all had one thing in common, with the exception of their wives: they didn't want to have sex with any girls over the age of 15.

As soon as Betty turned 15, she was sold to her American pimp in Kansas City. Betty's American pimp, Ramone, was heartless and the basic nature of his organization was an Asian connection.

Ramone was originally from Funk Town in Oakland, which at the time was a predominantly Chinese and Korean community near Lake Merritt.

Because of where he lived Ramone played mostly with Asian boys growing up. His best friends were Korean and they became his self-proclaimed Korean family.

As kids besides Bruce Lee, their hero were pimps and drug dealers. It appeared to them that the only realistic way for a fella from the hood to make money was through crime.

They aspired to one day have the women, the cars and the clothes, just like the ole' school Oakland pimps. Ramone and his crew called themselves P.A.K. -pimping all kinds.

Ramone became a specialist in the game, he was the only one who knew what to do with the hoes after they surpassed the age of 15, when they were considered to be worn out.

By the time Ramone was awarded custody of the girls, he would pimp them or re-sell them. He did something that not too many others could--very discreetly operate a human consignment store.

He could be very charming and could easily find a way to cheer a hoe up. (After he beat her ass).

Ramone made a lot of people happy, but he was a creep and he ruined a lot of lives. Despite Ramone's moral behaviors, if any pimp wanted to make money from the game and lots of it, he was the go-to person.

It was a little impressive to see how Ramone, a black man, conducted business in a circle of Asian businessmen. And, he could fluently speak Mandarin and Korean.

The biggest problem in Ramones' life were the Feds. They were on him like white on rice. It got worse, after a Kansas City congressman's daughter ran away with Ramone, at the age of 16.

The Congressman did everything in his power to have Ramone locked up. He was so determined to incarcerate Ramone that he began protesting with mothers against prostitution, outside of a Barber shop that Ramone invested in to appear like a legitimate businessman.

Ramone was so flashy with his fancy cars, clothes and jewelry that his appearance alone added fuel to the fire; he looked like a pimp. Finally Ramone slipped-up, got drunk and high and threw one of his hoes out of a window and that is when he was arrested.

After being arrested, Ramone told Betty where he kept all of his cash. He'd become fond of Betty, so much so that he even stopped making her go to work and had her living in the house with him.

Ramone gave Betty specific instructions to contact his lawyer and bail him out. He soon realized that he didn't have as much control over

14

Betty as he thought. She took the money but she never contacted his lawyer nor bailed him out. Instead she joined prosecutors and testified against Ramone.

Besides Betty's testimony, the D.A. couldn't find enough evidence to convict Ramone for pimping and pandering and in those days, the longest time pimps served was about 1 year. Betty's testimony didn't hold up in court because she was Ramones prostitute at one time. All of those boojie educated lawyers treated her like the criminal.

Then the congressman started throwing these words around- "Human Trafficking." Human Trafficking was new to the courts. Before Human Trafficking laws, pimps hardly ever went to jail; Prostitutes were the ones who committed the crime, so they were the one who served the time.

15

Prostitutes were afraid to speak out against their pimp or tell their story, because their work was illegal. Betty could have nailed Ramone as a sex offender, but she didn't reveal her age, in fear that the court would place her in a foster home; Betty just wanted to be free.

Betty's testimony against Ramone wasn't strong enough because of Ramones' lawyer. After finding out that Ramone was arrested, the Koreans hired a defense attorney. He was an ambitious, All-American White Boy, who kept calling Betty a whore.

Betty had 3 strikes against her, she was an Asian girl, a prostitute and she couldn't speak English clearly. No one in court could barely understand what she was saying. The court reporter kept asking her to repeat her testimony.

Betty would have been better off running away without testifying. The defenses argument, was that Betty was a bitter a girlfriend, upset that her boyfriend didn't marry her after finding out that she was a prostitute.

It was such a powerful argument. Ramones' attorney, convinced everyone in the courtroom, that Betty was a scorn woman who failed at executing an immigration scam.

"This woman is a Whore!" Ramones' Lawyer shouted.
"I object," yelled the prosecutor.
Ramones' Defense Lawyer continued to speak "She is a criminal who is too lazy to earn an honest living and she thought that she could come to the United States and illegally gain citizen ship, by marrying someone that she does not love." In the end, even the D.A. treated Betty with great contempt.

Ramone had so many political connections that he felt invincible; he believed that he would win his case. But his case became public and high profile. When the DA began naming some of Ramones criminal contacts, his political friends realized that too much information was being exposed. They knew, that if they didn't do something soon, his case could jeopardize their careers and their livelihood.

The politicians that flaunted around town with Ramone during the reign of his early years, did everything in their power to disassociate themselves from him and lock him up for good. So, they set a bail for him and allowed the Koreans to bail him out of jail. Once Ramone was released the police followed him everywhere. They tapped his phone and wired his house. It only took one day for the police to set Ramone up and frame him on some drug manufacturing charges.

When he went back to court, they also up-held old charges from when he got drunk and threw one of his hoes out of a window. Finally, after hustling for 13yrs, Ramone was locked up and sent to the Fed's for 20yrs.

Betty had been long gone. As soon as the Koreans bailed Ramone out of jail she disappeared. That must have been when she used Ramones' money and ran off to California. Where, she started her own business and a new life.

Joy, or "Betty", had been on the run for a little over 2 years. She was around 17 years old when she ran away. After she changed her name and purchased a new I.D., she took a six-month esthetics course.

Betty started a brand new life in San Francisco, which was her fatal mistake. At first no one knew where she was. We all assumed that she'd moved back with her family in China. Had she done her research, she would have went back to China.

What she didn't know was that her pimp Ramone was mostly every balling pimp in the Bay Area's closet contact to Nepal, Mexico, China and Brazil, just to name a few. When Betty screwed him, she screwed the "chuch". Now it was time for her to get screwed and I was the screwdriver.

Most girls believed that no runaway could last longer than 1 year without her pimp. Either she would end up dead or be a cast away and mattressed.

At this point, I was so ambitious that despite how young and sweet Betty seemed and as much as she didn't deserve the fate that awaited her, I had an insatiable will to conquest.

The moment that I found Betty, I felt that I was finally doing something important, something that would gain me real notoriety.

20

I secretly admired how this young teen was brave enough to flee her Simon Legree and start her own business. My actions weren't personal, however, this was my time to run a stable on a grand scale.

I remembered my years as a young girl in East Oakland. Back then I never imagined being a part of a million dollar operation, traveling, driving fancy cars, wearing the most expensive designer clothes and lavish jewelry. Seems like it was only yesterday that I was hanging out with Fred and the gang.

East Oakland

"Let go of her neck!" I tugged at Marcus' arms but I wasn't strong enough to loosen the tight grip he had around Unique's throat.

The oohs and aah's from Fred weren't obliging. Fred was amused by violence, but it wasn't his fault. The biggest edification of Fred's bungling school day was watching another 12-year-old boy choke the life out of an innocent 12-year-old girl.

"Shut up Fred! Don't egg him on! Why don't you help me stop him?" I shouted at Fred.

Marcus was a skinny kid, but tall for his age, already 5'10" at 12 years old. If you looked closely, you could see that his upper torso leaned slightly toward the left due to a birth defect that he had called Scoliosis of the spine.

For the most part, he was handsome. He looked like any other kid, except for when he was tired. Because when he was tired, he would drag himself around and lean over.

No matter how much Marcus fit in socially or how good his grades were, he still had an angry streak. His deep insecurity about "being crippled", as he would call it, would sometimes cause him to get very short tempered. He could be real bipolar at times.   I turned away from Fred who was only about 4'10". Despite the fact that he and Marcus looked like Sonny and Cher when they stood next to one another, they were inseparable.

I continued to reason with Marcus. "Marcus just let her go!" As I pleaded for Marcus to stop choking Unique, I found that my voice was drowned out by a much more important cry of an aching community. A hood that wept out like a newborn baby in the form of weeping that resembled sirens, wino's arguing, screeching tires and loud hip-hop music.

For us, it wasn't the joyful noise of marching bands and Easter parades, not even sentimental sounds of children playing and laughing. No, we typically heard dogs barking, gunshots, car alarms and gangs fighting.

I was competing with a disquiet, which revealed itself through the horridness of violent pitchy tunes. Notes, that when heard as often as they are heard in this neighborhood, would cause even Mariah Carey to go tone deaf.

I wish I could say that I was surprised at Marcus' behavior or that I was uncomfortable witnessing such acts of violence. However, Marcus choking Unique was just another day in East Oakland, California. Except in this case, unlike the other culprits, Marcus didn't intend to kill Unique; he was hurting her to scare her, maybe.

24

Finally, after Fred's first attempt at asking Marcus to stop, Marcus let her go. As Unique's dangling feet hit the ground, she belted out, "Punk Nigga!" I was surprised. Unique clearly knew that she was no match for Marcus; still, he did not intimidate her.

Unique was gasping for air and caressing her throat while, simultaneously cursing at Marcus. He backed away facing her,   "Shut up you black monkey!" Marcus yelled as he spit down at the ground near Unique's feet. He never turned his back until he saw that Unique had slightly calmed down.

Fred reached down to grab his backpack while using his other hand to visor the California sun. He'd gotten so excited during the brawl that he had dropped all of his things.

Marcus walked on ahead in a passionate rage. Fred power walked close behind him trying to keep up, as if Marcus was his hero. I patted Unique on the back and helped her collect her things from off of the ground.

As we continued to walk home, I made an attempt to comfort Unique. I found myself trying to remind Unique that Marcus really was a good guy. "Don't pay him any attention, Unique, he's tripping today. He ain't never flashed like that on you before. He sees you as his potna. He's just got a lot on his mind that's all." By that time, Marcus and Fred were walking far ahead of us.

Marcus, Fred, Unique and I were all in the 6Th grade; back then 6Th grade was the last year of elementary school. Usually, we would walk home from school together and generally we got along, but today Unique said something that made Marcus extremely upset.

I can't even remember the content of the conversation, or what made Marcus detonate and grab Unique's throat. Yet, still despite what I thought about our environment, deep down I grieved a little inside because no one helped her or called the cops. It gave me a feeling of hopelessness.

Cars zoomed past us, with people inside who looked neither to the left nor right. The knocked up dope-fiends who were sitting at the bus stop across the street just watched on with no interference. Their only mission in life was hitchhiking their way back to euphoria through their next hit, by any means possible.

I didn't want Marcus to get into any kind of trouble, but I wanted someone to care. Although we were children, these cats were so used to hearing about victims of all ages being injured or murdered that their instinct to protect us was oxidized to nothing.

27

Almost every night on the evening news, there were reports of crime in our area; and every night, it seemed that the suspects had gotten younger and younger. Crimes consisted of robbery, rape, arson, drug dealing and prostitution- just to name a few.

Most of the adults in our neighborhood were working, tied up into their own lives and trying to keep their own kids off of drugs. Other adults were so afraid of the kids that they let the police deal with us.

Police were never around when we needed them. Half of the officers were overworked, much of their effort was spent fighting crime, volunteering as spokespersons for DARE or handing out traffic tickets.

The other half of the police force were like a feeble infection; they spent their time contaminating every living soul that was in their path. They were the biggest racists, killers, pimps and dealers in town and proud of it. I mean who could stop them? They were the police.

The lack of adult supervision and protection was unfortunate for Unique because she really was a good girl.

Marcus' abusive behavior towards Unique wasn't enough to prevent me from following him home after his vexation came to a standstill.

He split from Fred and waited for me at the stop light across the street. I hugged Unique, watched her walk off to her bus stop and started to cross the street. "Watch out!" Fred yelled.

A Ford Mustang with star wire rims and Vogue tires sped out into the intersection. The driver deliberately began spinning the car into synchronized, figure 8 patterns closely followed by whole, closed curves circles (or what we normally called Donuts). After about the fourth gyration, the blue 65 mustang dashed off leaving tire marks on the road and a trail of smoke. Fred was rooting and yelling, "Did y'all see that?! Did you see them donuts? That's gonna be me next year, wait and see!"

After the smoke cleared from the mustang, I hurried along across the street to meet up with Marcus.

As I cautiously continued to cross the street Marcus became impatient." C'mon Red-bone let's go! " Red-bone was Marcus's nickname for me. It means light-skinned girl.

At 12 years old I was very statuesque, my measurements were already 34-24-37. My mother was mixed with West Indian and Creole, which is probably where my light complexion derived and my father was African American.

I was very pretty and what cats in the hood called thick. I couldn't walk one block without some old man trying to get me in the car with him. Marcus was my protection from the wolves and I was not about to walk through the forest alone.

The four of us would wait for one another after school and walked most of the way together. Unique and Fred were neighbors and usually caught the same bus. Marcus and I both lived two blocks away from one another and would walk home together the rest of the way.

Marcus' attack on Unique, didn't cause me to think twice about easing back into my usual after school routine, of walking home with him. I thought that maybe I could talk some sense into him.

On the way home, I attempted to convince Marcus to make amends with Unique. I asked Marcus why he choked Unique, he answered.
"Man that rat! She needs to mind her business, she's

been going around talking about me and Cherise, you know I'm private and Cherise is so shy I don't want rumors to be spread around about her; it might hurt her feelings."

I couldn't help but feel envious towards Cherise. I couldn't believe he was that angry over a girl that he liked, a girl who wasn't me. "Let me get this clear, you choked my friend because you didn't want Cherise to get her feelings hurt? Unique is my only friend. If you would have told me in the first place, I would have talked with her about it." Marcus looked at me apologetically and said, "I'm sorry Kandi. Unique is my friend too. I will apologize to Unique tomorrow."

Marcus was the kind of guy that never really looked at the big picture. I warned him, "If she tells on you Marcus, it could jeopardize all that you've worked for. You know that there is a strong possibility that you'll get accepted into Charter School next year. Don't mess that up."

32

"You're right Kandi, I can't mess that up over some hood-rat. Cherise doesn't even like me anyway. She's just a tease!"

He began to say something else, a mumble under his breath that I couldn't understand. Then he belted out, "snobby bitch." Most girls in East Oakland seemed to have inherited disrespectful names; the same way we inherited poverty.

When we reached Marcus house, I watched him leap up the three steps from the sidewalk. As he pulled out his key, he looked down at me and asked, "Are you coming inside or what? My mom won't be home for another four hours."

Marcus waited at the front door, looking down at me with an impatient stare. I glared back and said "Well I think that I should be getting home, my mom is probably wondering where I am," Marcus just stood there staring at me. "What?" I asked.

Marcus continued looking down at me and said, "Kandi, you know that your mom doesn't care about where you are. She's probably at the club, at happy hour or something, looking for your new daddy. I guarantee that she calls you later drunk, lying, talking 'bout she's gotta work overtime." He was right, but I was still offended. "Oh, and your mother doesn't work overtime?" I asked.

Marcus quickly defended his mother, "Yes she does, except the only difference between my mother and yours is that my mother is really at work when she says she is. Listen, Red-bone, I don't want to argue with you. Please come inside? Let me fix you a sandwich."

He looked like one of those lost, hungry puppies that you find strolling throughout the neighborhood without a nametag. Like a compassionate dog lover, I wanted to rescue him.

We went inside the house and Marcus lead me straight into his room. I sat down on the bed as Marcus turned on the television. "Oh! Kandi, look at this! It's the episode of Pinky and the Brain that I was telling you about." "Marcus, is it the episode where they're *not* trying to take over the world? Because if not, I've already seen it."

Marcus sat down beside me and started rubbing my breast. "You don't have to get sarcastic for me to think that you are smart, Kandi." I tapped his hand, smiled and said, "They try to take over the world in every episode…I'm just saying!"

We looked at each other and laughed, then we started kissing, then more touching and then he pulled my jeans down as I helped. Despite our age, this wasn't the first time that we'd ever had sex together.

In a perfect world, people get married before they even think about having sex. They have children, a house with a picket fence, two cars and a dog.

In my world, Marcus wasn't even my boyfriend. I thought that when Marcus finally felt the need to call someone his girlfriend, I would be first in line. To my bewilderment, he asked Cherise.

Cherise was another girl in our sixth grade class who was the teacher's pet. Her mother was on the PTA board and her mother intimidated everyone.

When Marcus asked Cherise to be his girlfriend,

Cherise told him that she didn't want to be his girlfriend, only his friend. She said that she needed to focus on getting her education. She told Marcus that he should focus on his education, too.

Marcus really admired Cherise and bragged about her ambition. Whenever I spoke about having a better life and growing up to be someone important, Marcus would laugh and say, "It's too late for you Kandi."

At school, Marcus spent most of his time catering to Cherise's mom. She thought that he was the sweetest kid. It guessed that Marcus was so infatuated with Cherise because she was from a two-parent home, well-manicured, and goal-oriented. I think that's what he liked about her.

After Cherise found out that Marcus liked her, she started inviting him places. They went to the movies, to church, to baseball games, she even took him to see the Nutcracker in San Francisco, her parents would chaperone.

All of the faculty members at our school thought highly of Marcus. He was a good student. Marcus always volunteered in the Principal's office. He loved sports and was great at playing drums. The Marcus that I knew, was a thug whose luck prevented him from being in Juvenile hall.

Cherise had everything, including Marcus, but she seemed to spend a lot of time questioning Marcus about our friendship.

She would often be cruel toward me. If she saw me speaking with him on the playground, *"Marcus!"* She would call. Cherise would bat her eyes smile and say, *"come here let me tell you what happened to me at the 49ers game."* She would always yell out something cool and interesting and he would surely go running to her.

Cherise knew that he was hers outside on the playground, but she didn't know that after school, he would seduce me in his bedroom.

The look in his eyes and his apparent pleasure, was empowering for me. I found my purpose. I found something that I was good at.

I had good grades in school. But, good grades didn't matter to me. How I performed in school, didn't seem matter to anyone else or make a difference in anyone else's life.

Once, I told a teacher that I wanted to be a news journalist and she told me that I would never succeed at it. "You're pretty," she said, "but your lips are too big. You just don't have 'the look' for television." I may not have the look for television, but right here, right now I have the look for satisfying a boy.

The only time that I felt important, was when Marcus would beg, to have sex with me. I would think, I'm in control now. I have something that someone else wants and needs.

"Turn around!" Marcus demanded."

"No, Why?" I asked.

"I want to try something new, don't start asking questions, Kandi, it's a turnoff!"

I was offended, "Turn off? No! Get off of me, I'm leaving!"   Marcus slapped me so hard, that a red hand print tattooed the side of my yellow skin for a moment. "Shut up slut!" He roared.
He pushed me on the bed, threw me on my stomach and shoved himself inside of me. "Marcus stop,

you're hurting me. Stop, that hurts me Marcus, stop it!" I struggled with no success. "Stop Marcus, NO!" I yelled. I didn't feel so empowered anymore. I didn't know how to feel. I was always taught that 'No means No.' the confusing part for me was, did it mean no after you've already said yes?

I'd said yes earlier but, I really wanted Marcus to stop at that moment. He was holding me down and he was hurting me, but I was confused because he was my best friend. Marcus moaned out, "Oh, I'm Cumming!"

I had semen dripping down my butt and I was thinking, *I didn't authorize this.* I was mentally disoriented, from what had happened to me. Meanwhile, the sound of television commercials echoed distantly in the room. We were both quiet.

Marcus got up and began to wipe himself off. He was standing at the edge of the bed. He nudged my foot and said, "Kandi why you gotta be so dramatic?" I didn't respond. He asked, "I'm hungry are you hungry?"   Marcus threw me a washcloth, before I could respond. "Clean up, I'm going to go make us some peanut butter and jelly sandwiches."

We left Marcus' house after we ate. The walk home was quiet and lonely, even though Marcus wouldn't stop ranting about something to do with Charter school lottery.

I just wanted to be home. The streetlights were on already and I needed to make it back.

Near the stop sign at the end of my block, Marcus kissed me on the cheek and said,

"Meet me at the corner store in the morning. Please be there at 7:30! Don't be late." "I won't," I replied. "Oh and Kandi, don't get the bright idea of telling any counselors at school our business." "I'm not going to say anything Marcus."

Marcus kissed me on the cheek;   I looked at him and wiped my face. I was beginning to resent Marcus. I wanted to say something to upset him. "I know when we were in the 4th grade, that 6th grader Urethra was fondling you. That's how you lost your virginity." I wanted to rekindle in him feelings of betrayal and endangerment. I wanted to make him feel how he'd just made me feel. "Actually, that is not how I lost my virginity, Kandi. I lost my virginity, when my babysitter and her boyfriend started molesting me from the age of 4 until the age of 8. You already know that and you know how it makes me feel to even think about it, so stop talking about my virginity. I should have never told you."

Suddenly, I deeply regretted purposefully hurting my friend's feelings. "I won't mention it anymore, Marcus."

He watched me walk to my porch from the corner. Before I walked through the door I waved bye to Marcus. He blew me a kiss and turned away.

When I got into my house, I rushed to answer the telephone, which was on the third ring.

"Hello" I answered.
"Hello Kandi, it's mommy I have to work an extra shift, my co-worker called out sick. There's no one here to cover her shift. Make sure the doors and windows are locked before you go to bed and heat up the leftovers in the microwave. I'll be home around 3am." "OK mom, I love you." I said and waited for her to respond. "OK Kandi don't forget to lock the doors, you know that you can be irresponsible at times. Bye-bye!" Mom replied.
I hung up the phone and sighed in relief. I had made it home before my mother and that was a good thing; because, I had no explanation for where I'd been or what I had been doing for the past three hours.

After finishing my homework, I was struck with an insatiable boredom. I really didn't feel like speaking to anyone on the phone but I was lonely. Usually mom and I would wash dishes after dinner, well, if she wasn't drunk.

When mom did come home sober, we shared great moments. We would watch TV and sing some of our favorite songs. Tonight, there was no laughing, no dinner cooking, nothing to clean and no one to sing to.

My mother was a smart woman. She was originally from Shreveport, Louisiana. She moved to California with some slick-talking city boy from Palo Alto.

Mom thought that he was going to turn her into a movie star... That is what he told her and that is what she believed.

My mother was an amazing singer, but she was the biggest sucker for love known to mankind. Every stupid decision that she ever made, stimulated from some man feeding her with false promises.

The type that always tried to change emasculated men, my mother always had a bum boyfriend. She just could not be single.

At first she vowed to never let them move in with us. My mother always criticized our next-door neighbor, because it seemed as though a new man was living with her every six months.

My mother would say, "That's a shame, that woman has all of those strange men around those kids. She can't keep her legs closed to save her life. I would never let no grown man live with me."

Then it happened- at first, men could only spend the night. Until, one was finally clever enough to realize that alcohol and fear of being lonely, were my mother's real weaknesses. He would get my mom drunk and promise to marry her. She looked so stupid, going around telling everyone that she was engaged without a ring on her finger.

The loser didn't even work. He told my mom that he hurt his shoulder, working security for the singer Alexander O'Neal down in Los Angeles. He said that the crowd had gotten so frantic, that they rushed him and dislocated his shoulder.

The giveaway, was that he loved to break-dance. Whenever my mother's boyfriend got drunk enough, he would go as far as getting on the ground and spinning on his back and shoulder, dancing the helicopter.

He told mom that he would introduce her to "Alex," so that she could start her singing career.

But first they had to wait for "Alex," to get back from is tour- As if he knew the man on a first name basis.

He and my mother were constantly arguing, because he would disappear for days at a time. Things around the house would turn up missing. My mother would hide her jewelry and car keys. I finally said what we were both thinking,
"I think that he is on drugs, mom."
"Shut up and stay in a child's place," she ordered.

My mother never cared deeply enough about things around the house being stolen. No, her final limit was when the creep had the nerve to get my mother drunk and asked if he could do a threesome with her and me. I never saw him again. I think my mother blamed me for her "fiancé's" attraction toward me and she never forgave me for it.

After my mother broke up with her "fiancé" she stopped coming home. I saw her watching me strangely and she would always say,
"You're looking fat! Your butt is sticking out like a horse."

My mother began dating a new guy about a month later and I wasn't seeing her very often. This time, she decided to go over his house and keep him away from me. I missed her. I sat there in my mother's apartment, all alone and I knew that she wasn't coming home.

As I sat their lonely, I couldn't understand why my mother seemed to love and accept love, from everyone except me.

I felt bored and forsaken, so I decided to, call Unique.
"Hello may I speak to Unique?"
"Hey Kandi what's up? It's me!"
"What's up Unique? What are you doing?" I asked,

49

Unique answered "Nothing, I'm bored! I'm just sitting here, playing Barbie, with my little sister. She keeps putting the dolls on top of each other making them do the nasty. By the way, what was up with your boyfriend today?"

"He's not my boyfriend Unique; he's just a boy."

"Well whatever! Excuse me then, Cherise's boyfriend- ha! You know that it's because of Cherise that Marcus choked me today? He did it because I told Fred that Cherise is ugly and I didn't know why Marcus liked Cherise. Fred went back and told Marcus." Unique continued talking. "But for real Kandi, she is so plain. She's a nerd and have you seen her fingernails? She bites her nails. Gross!"

I began reasoning with Unique, I said. "Unique you know that Fred is going to go back and tell Marcus, they are friend." I tried to reconcile the situation, but I was still upset that Marcus choked Unique, for ridiculing Cherise.

Unique explained slowly and clearly.
"Marcus hates me Kandi. He came into my class
today during silent reading, while volunteering as
an office-aide. He had to deliver my teachers mail.
When I looked up at him he flapped his ears and
puffed out his cheeks, insinuating that I looked like
a monkey."
"You don't look like a monkey Unique." I said.
"I'm not so sure about that Kandi. I have to go. My
mom said, that I have to get ready for bed."

"Okay Unique I'll see you tomorrow."

I hung up the phone with recurring thoughts
of my mother floating through my head. I tried
calling her back at work but there was no answer. I
turned on the television, laid down on the sofa and
fell asleep.

Chapter Two

Chapter II

At 7:27am I found myself jogging toward the corner store. Something from my book bag was poking me in the side. I was sure that my ruler was poking me, but I only had three minutes to meet Marcus at the corner store and I wasn't about to stop running.

Every morning I rushed to meet Marcus. Meeting Marcus before school, meant that I would be able to eat breakfast and lunch. His mother always gave him a breakfast and lunch allowance that he usually shared with me.

Marcus and I had known each other since Kindergarten. Marcus was my only friend for most of my life, until Unique transferred into our school in the fourth grade.

Marcus had always protected me ever since I could remember. In kindergarten, some girls huddled around me hitting me in the face, pulling my hair and taunting me. "Bubble butt, bubble butt, you look like a donkey!" they teased. Marcus was right there to defend me.

Marcus was the first person to tell me that I was pretty. He said, that the reason why he liked me so much was, because I was the best reader in class. Marcus use to complement me and say that, I was the smartest girl that he knew.

By the time we reached second grade, Marcus noticed that I never ate at lunchtime. Every lunch hour I went straight to the playground. He came over to the slide holding a brown paper bag "I'm not hungry; you want the rest of my lunch? I have a Twinkies, some punch and half of a turkey sandwich." He handed me the bag before I could answer and ran off to play basketball.

I was curious to know why such a popular boy, was so interested in being my friend. He was curious to know why I never ate at lunchtime.

I eventually told Marcus the reason why I never ate at school. I never at school lunch, because the kids teased me when I ate it. One girl even said that I was so poor, that I was living off of pennies. It hurt my feelings.

Marcus shared his secret about being diagnosed with Scoliosis and how he would force himself to stand up straight even though the pain was excruciating.

"Eventually I just got used to the pain," he said.

He also shared with me intimate secrets of how his mom's best friend, who was also his babysitter, would force him to perform sexual acts with her. He was as young as 4 years old. By the time Marcus was 8 years old he was having full intercourse with his babysitter. I remember peeing on her when it was time for me to ejaculate." He would say.

One day his babysitter's boyfriend walked in and caught him sucking his babysitter's breast and broke Marcus arm.

Later that night, he came into the room where Marcus was sleeping and forced Marcus to perform oral sex on him, "You want to suck something Lil' Nigga? Suck on this!"

A homemade sling cradled Marcus' arm and when he reached home Marcus' mom interrogated Marcus until he finally confessed. Marcus' mom had her best friend and her boyfriend placed in jail.

I remembered Marcus coming to school in the

second grade with a sheet tied around his broken arm.

The couple only served 6 months in jail, because providing evidence in a child maltreatment case is one of the most difficult milestones to overcome. During a four month time frame Marcus' story changed 17 times. The courts were convinced that something happened, but they just couldn't prove, what exactly.

Marcus told me all of his secrets so freely. I used to think, it was because he valued me highly as a person. I thought that he treasured our friendship. I now know, that Marcus told me those things because he didn't think much of me. He thought that I was as destitute, as his pathetic past.

7:32am I saw Marcus standing outside of the corner store from the end of the block. He yelled, "Hurry up Red-bone!"
He was holding his stomach laughing at me, because I was running. By the time I reached him he was hunched over laughing.
"You're sweating Kandi, you didn't have to run; it's not that serious. You're about to catch a hernia straggling for food. You are so sloppy! I got you a donut and some milk, and here," Marcus handed me a five-dollar bill. "My mom gave me some extra money this morning. I told her that I needed extra money to buy some supplies."

I was still feeling weird and confused about Marcus attacking me, but I really appreciated the fact that he was considerate enough to make sure I had lunch money. "Thanks Marcus!" I said.
"No problem Kandi. You're my girl. You're the smartest girl I know, well, you used to be. Anyway. In any case, you still gotta have your brain food."

On the way to school, I was really silent. Marcus was jabbering about something the entire walk. Then his voice faded back in. All I heard was, "speaking of the Charter school, the Lottery is today!" By that time we were on the school campus near my class, I just wanted to ditch him and find Unique. "I'll cross my fingers for you Marcus; I know you'll get in." I winked at Marcus and walked to my class. I heard a voice echo in my direction, it was Cherise. "Why are you always in my boyfriend's face?" The red frames from Cherise's glasses made it easy to recognize my accuser from the corner of my eye. I was shocked at Cherise's choice of words, **her boyfriend?** Who had she turned into? And who did she think she was talking to?

"He's my friend, Cherise, that's all. As a matter of fact, he's just your friend too, so why are you sweating me?" Unique walked up behind me, "Yeah why are you sweating her four-eyes?"

Unique was rolling her neck so hard that one of her braids hit me in the face. "Come on girl let's go to class, we don't have time for this Rat!" Unique tugged at my sweater and we walked off to our classes. "I'll see you at recess." Unique said to Cherise as the bell rang.

"Girl, what was up with that nerd? She's got her nerve coming at you like that." Said Unique as we went off to our classes to learn, nothing.

The end of the school day couldn't have come soon enough. I held onto the $5 that Marcus gave me, just in case my mother had to work overtime. My mother had been working so much lately that I felt like I lived alone. I definitely felt like I was raising myself and I hadn't seen my dad... Not, since I called over his house and cursed out my stepmother.

I didn't have anything against my stepmother at the time, I was just really hungry that night and there was no food in the house. My mother wasn't home, so I called my dad, out of extreme desperation; He wasn't even home anyway.

My stepmother must have told him that I called because it was one of the few days that he came over our house. When I saw him through the peephole I thought I saw a ghost.

I opened the door and he stood in the doorway about 6 feet tall. I let him into the apartment. I plopped down on the sofa and stared at him.

My dad began his complaint, "Why are you calling my house disrespecting my wife Kandi?"

"I'm hungry daddy, I need some money."

"Where is your mama?"

"I don't know daddy."

"Well you can come over my house and get something to eat, Donna cooked dinner."

"Your wife hates me daddy, I'm not coming over your house."

"Well I'll see you later."

Just like that my dad walked out and closed the door, again. I shook my head at my past and knit brows at my future. Maybe I should try to go to a charter school, I thought.

After school, I walked across the schoolyard to the bleachers near the school exit, I only saw Unique and Fred. They were there waiting for me. I wondered where Marcus was.

Fred excitedly announced, "Did you hear? Marcus got picked in the lottery! He's going to that charter school next year. Dang I wish they would have picked my name."

Fred looked down for a moment. He knew that going to the charter school was his only chance of making it out of the ghetto.

"Well Fred," Unique said, "you can always be a rapper; you got any rhyming skills?"

We all laughed. "That's the fastest way for you to get that mustang that you want. Let's go to the store. I want to get a score bar." Unique suggested.

On the way to the store Fred kept ranting on about selling weed. Fred told us that his older cousin recently bought the car of his dreams, a Ford Mustang… "All from slanging dope. It's so easy, look at all of these fiends around us y'all! I could have sold 5 rocks by now."

Unique frowned her face, "Rocks? I thought that you said you were going to sell weed Fred."

"I'm going to do whatever I gotta do Unique. I am about to go in this store and steal some candy right now. Kandi cover for me."

We went into the store and Fred started stuffing candy down his pants leg. Unique and I distracted the clerk. "What's up Mohammad?" I asked. "You like my new pants? How do you think they fit? Do I look good?"

Mohammad was a young Persian man, maybe in his 20's. He had only been in the country for about 5 months. He spoke English fluently but he had a heavy accent. Mohammad loved black girls.

"Yes girl, if you were in my country I would have you as one of my wives. You have a face like the moon."

Unique covered her mouth and chuckled. "A face like the moon?" Unique repeated and couldn't stop laughing.

Fred slipped out of the door and even though I was free to go, I wanted to play with Mohammad's head a little more. So I said,

"Well if you'll have me, I will be your wife now. If you tasted some of this, you'll be seeing the moon and the stars baby."

Mohammad loved flirting with me. "Oh my God baby! I would kiss every part of your body and make you feel good."

Unique couldn't stop chuckling "come on Moon, I mean Kandi, we got to go!"

Outside Fred was separating our treats. "What took you so long? You know I got to be at the bus stop soon. If I miss my bus, my mom is going to kill me."

Unique was apologetic "Sorry Fred it was Kandi,

she taking longer and longer to flirt with Mohammad, I think that she likes him,"

"No I don't" I snatched my chocolate bar out of Fred's hand, waved bye and parted with my friends.

I really wanted to see Marcus. I wanted to hear the good news from his mouth. I decided to walk down his block on my way home.

I saw him. There Marcus was, walking into the house with his Mother and Cherise right beside him. He was holding her book bag. I could tell that he really liked Cherise, but this was supposed to be our moment. I thought he would have been happy to celebrate with me.

They were already inside when I passed the front door. I could hear them celebrating and laughing from the sidewalk.

Through the window, I could see Marcus's Mom in the kitchen starting a meal. Marcus and Cherise were in the living room, working on their homework. I felt a pain in my heart and in my side, similar to the ruler that was poking through my backpack. Unlike the ruler, this feeling was emotional.

I don't know what it was, but something made me turn around and walk back toward the store. Maybe it was to pass Marcus house again, just to make sure I wasn't dreaming. Maybe, I was subconsciously trying to erase what I'd just seen by retracing my footsteps.

Once I started walking. I couldn't stop. I found myself back at the corner store staring into the eyes of Mohammad.

Mohammad smiled and said, "Look who it is, my girl! What brings you back honey? Where are your friends?" I was there back with Mohammad, so I was going to make the best of it. I looked at Mohammad and said, "I had to shake them. They don't know how to keep up with a big girl like me but I bet you do." Mohammad always talked a good game, but he had a look of fear in his eyes. He was lost for words.

That's when I realized, that all of those times that I'd seen Mohammad, he was seriously only flirting.

Mohammad was hesitant at first. He didn't want to take things further than a conversation about sex. I had to say something to break the tension. I asked him to show me the restroom. He told me that his restroom wasn't for public use.

"Please Mohammad, it's me Kandi, let me use the bathroom."

Mohammad stared at me for a long time; he gave me a real grown up look, the way your teacher looks at you when she is trying to put you in your place. "Okay, make it fast. If my boss catches you behind the register it could jeopardize my job." I was so embarrassed. I was hurt and ashamed. My mind was blank and when I went into the bathroom, I felt like I had been urinating for an eternity.

Mohammad knocked on the door. "Come out of there, you have to go now."

I replied, "I'm washing my hands, I'll be out in a second." I turned off the water and opened the bathroom door." Where are the paper towels?" I said, as I looked Mohammad in the eyes, stood closer in front of him and begin wiping my hand on his shirt. I began to rub his stomach and then I unbuckling his pants. I started fondling him.

He looked at me and said, "Oh my goodness baby, please don't stop!" I looked at Mohammad with a serious look in my eye. I placed his hand on my butt and said, "You know how this goes, if you want more, you have to pay to play. Give me $100 and I'm yours."

He told me to wait in the bathroom. Mohammad went to the front of the store; he put up the sign, WILL BE BACK SOON, and locked the door.

After closing the store Mohammad went into the register and took out five, $20 bills. All that he could think of was getting sexual favors from me, the thickest girl in the neighborhood.

When he came back into the bathroom, I took the money out of his hands, got down on my knees, closed my eyes and opened my mouth. I don't know what made me go into the store or ask him for money. I don't even know what made me demand $100, it all just happened.

I got what I wanted and he got what he wanted. I made a difference in someone else's life. I made him content in that moment, I was good at making him happy. I got paid more money than I'd ever had in my life,

The money really didn't matter to me. Pleasing a man made me feel validated. After Marcus betrayed me, I felt worthless. The $100 that Mohammad paid me, made me feel valuable. It was official- the first encounter of my long-term career as a harlot.

Chapter Three

Chapter III

The past was over, I would sometime daydream when I found myself in a position that I really didn't want to be in. I thought about the things that I'd done, the things that I could have done, the things that I should have done. On this day I found myself in a "shoulda—woulda - coulda" conflict. I sat there at the mucky looking glass table, staring at a stack of forms stapled together and full of personal questions.

Job Corps

A feeling of isolation confined me. It dawned on me that up until that moment, I'd never met anyone, who wanted to know that much about me; *what's your name? What's your date of birth? First pet's name?* I was about to "lose it" from all of the reading and writing of personal questions and answers.

I could picture myself sitting there, with the tip of the pen in my mouth, looking up into the air allowing my mind to drift back to 1997.

Four years had gone by since I'd last seen Marcus or Unique. Marcus' mom decided to move closer to Montclair where Marcus was attending his new school. Meanwhile, Unique's mother and father had reconciled their marriage and bought a house in Antioch; which was a 45 min suburb

North- East of East Oakland.

My mother's new boyfriend, had gotten the bright idea that Job Corps was a great head start for a 16-year-old teenage girl. He figured that I probably wouldn't graduate high school, let alone get into college.

I started cutting school so often that I was probably still reading at a six-grade level. I only met my mother's boyfriend a few times, but I knew that he didn't have any kids and that he didn't want anything to do with me.

Sending me to job corps was also my mother's way of avoiding jail time. I had cut school so often that the truancy officers fined my mother and threatened to send her to jail, if she didn't pay. My mother's defense, was telling the court that I was irrepressible.

I must admit, I did stop coming home at night. If it weren't for the court fines, my mother wouldn't have even noticed. She herself, only came home a couple of nights a month.

I was home alone quite often. That was because my mother's boyfriend lived in Vallejo, which was about 30 miles North of East Oakland.

If it wasn't for the extra money that I made from Mohammad, I would have slept in the dark. My mother stopped paying the utility bills and I quickly learned how to pay the light bill with the money that I earned.

My mother spent most nights at her boyfriend's house. She was oblivious to my actions. She couldn't discipline me because she was never home. Whenever she did 'pop-up' at home, I was nowhere to be found. Which meant, that she would rummage around the neighborhood looking for me.

Before I was sent to Job Corps, Mohammad got fired for trying to seduce another girl, an 11yr old girl. When the little girl went home and told her father, her father went into the store, beat up Mohammad and smashed all of the store's front windows.

Until then, the corner store was where I spent most of my days. I would watch TV, while waiting for him in the back of the store. I would give him sexual favors during his breaks.

Mohammed's payment became less and less. Which meant it got harder and harder for me to keep the lights on and eat.

I hustled up one or two tricks by putting on the shortest, tightest dress that I could find from my mother's closet and walked down the street.   It wouldn't take long for some old man to drive up next to me and offer a ride. After accepting the ride, I would usually have to initiate the first move to assure them that I wasn't 5.0.

I was shy, so I rehearsed a script, a personal code to say to the trick. I did all that I could to help them feel comfortable. I would say, "I am so HOT!" Real sexy and slow and then I would begin taking off my top. After that, the trick would pull over and we would negotiate prices, $100 for a blow job.

I loved pulling a Mexican trick. Especially, one that just got to the states and didn't speak any English. Those were the ones that would just get me in the car, hand me a hundred dollar bill, pull out their penis then push my head down, nut & go.

79

That is how I kept the lights on when my mother stopped paying the bills and feeding me. My mother didn't care, and if she didn't have section 8 to pay the rent, I would have had to worry about more than the lights being cut off. I would have had to worry about being homeless.

After some pimps tried to kidnap me, I had gotten really dependent on Mohammad. I made the mistake of befriending a bottom bitch of the biggest Mack on East 14 St. I told her that I was making $100 per blow job and she started hating. She just started yelling at me for no reason.

The working lady, a gutter snake that could never be trusted, looked at me with a cold stare and hissed, "$100! Bitch you making movie star money. I'm the top hoe in the area and I'm only getting $20. It's 'cause of you young fresh meat, that the game is getting twisted… nice and tight huh?"

After that, all of the other hoes started acting shady. Two hoes jumped me one day when I was coming from school. Then a pimp chased me four blocks down High St. one night trying to gorilla me into his stable. He ran up behind me and threw me down on the ground. He was trying to carry me into a white van when I scratched him and ran. He chased full speed behind me and kept saying, "That's the game bitch you just looked at me in the eye now you are mine."

I lost him when I hopped a fence; he stopped chasing me because he didn't want to mess up his perm. I was afraid and I no longer wanted to be seen on the blade. Oakland was way too dangerous; I stayed as low key as possible.

One girl from my school was trying to talk me into joining some new dating website on the internet but in those days I thought that it was weird to post pictures of yourself on-line, for complete strangers to be in your business.

I needed Mohammad and he knew it, he began to treat me like a stooge. The last time I saw him, he told me that he only had $10 in cash. I decided to stop going to see him, thinking that he would miss me- suffer without me; you know, to show him a lesson. That is when he tried to flirt with the other little girl.

Remember the girl, whose father beat up Mohammad? What Fred told me, was that the little girl asked him where he kept the suckers, meaning lollipops, Mohammad pulled out his penis and told her, "I've got the sucker you need right here and free lollipops for practice." The little girl ran home and told her dad. Her dad came back into the store, broke Mohammad's jaw in four places and stabbed him in the balls. That was the end of Mohammad.

High School was a complete waste of time. The girls were all having complementary sex. The boys were immature and everyone was extremely irresponsible. There was a bad epidemic of crabs spreading around. So severe, that there were reports of crab sightings; spotted on the toilet seats in the girl's bathroom.

Their mother and Gangsta Rap Music were raising most of the boys. Every girl, in every song, went by the infamous name Bitch. Marcus was no longer there to protect me from the other kids.

It was difficult for me, but I still didn't have it as bad as some of the new girls. The girls who transferred into our school districts from other cities, would get harassed and jumped almost every day.

Fred transferred to the same school as me.

He spent most of his time behind the main building, smoking weed with his new crew. His friends were two lanky trouble starters. The three of them together were the neighborhood marijuana dealers. They called themselves Sacks 3, insinuating that they had 'sacks of weed and it was 3 of them'.

Selling weed was Fred's strategy for buying the 5.0 mustangs that he had long been eyeing. Fred never did make enough money for that mustang and instead, he bought a GM Cutlass. The music in that car was so loud, that the car window would rattle. He even had speakers in the front grill of the car.

I tried cutting school with Fred a few times but I hated the way that smoking weed made me feel. He had gotten his hands on some kind of weed called kryptonite. After getting high from it, we would laugh uncontrollably and fall asleep.

On Friday nights, I would hang out with Fred and go to the sideshow. The sideshow is an East Oakland tradition. Kids from East Oakland have been keeping this custom for decades. A display of decorated classic cars and the best car stunts the eyes have ever seen. The Sideshow is completely amazing and completely illegal.

When the police show up, everyone gets in their cars and speed away to new location. Once they drive to a different part of town, they start it up, all over again.

While at the sideshow, Fred would go to look at the cars. I would be trying to pick up a stupid boy that would pay. Fred was really my only friend, when it came to socializing.

Even though, I hated smoking weed, I would still smoke it because Fred always had it. One time,

85

after smoking with Fred, I passed out and woke up in the back of the school at 2:00am and Fred was gone. I walked home vowing to never smoke weed again.

During school hours I found myself walking around the neighborhood, trying to avoid school security and my mother. One day as I was walking, I heard a man call from his porch.   "Hey Lil' girl, can I trust you to go to the store and grab me a Hav-a-Tampa cigar?"

He seemed to be looking right at me. I asked myself the question, why can't he go to the store himself? I leaned over the fence and answered him. "Yeah I'll go to the store for you, but it will cost you $5."
He laughed and said, "Wow you kids are getting more and more expensive; I remember the days when I could pay a kid fifty cents."

86

"Why can't you just go to the store yourself?" I asked.
He stuck his hands out in front of him but not too far, trying to be discrete. He was reaching out for his chair. Then it dawned on me- I stared him up and down. I realized that his blue and white plaid robe, didn't match his green shirt and his yellow Cal Bears sweats. One of his slippers was grey and the other one was black. "Your blind aren't you?" I asked. He sat down on his porch chair and said, "That's what they say."

I was curious to know, how he knew, that I was walking by and that I was a girl. As soon as I attempted to inquire, he interrupted and said, "I saw you walking."
Now I was confused, "But I thought you said that you were blind and from the looks of your clothes you definitely are blind, so how did you know that I was a girl?"

He laughed and explained to me that every now and then, not often, he could see things. This time when his sight had come back he ran outside and saw me. "I'm what they call partially blind."

"Okay, so you've come this far, why not keeping walking to the store or ask one of those Mexican labor guys across the street? They will go to the store for you for $5." I was only picking on him.

Mexican immigrants, would stand in line across the street from his house. Waiting for a decent gigs.

"Sometimes they go to the store for me, if no one has picked them up for work by noon. Normally that's the time when they figure that they probably won't get a gig. They come here, to see if I need anything. I send them to the store to buy a case of beer and some cigars. They take half, I take half, I give them a few dollars and were even; an eye for an eye, right?"

I admired him from the beginning, even in his helpless state, the old man found a way to be humorous, cleverly sarcastic and resourceful.

The old man was perhaps in his sixties, no older than sixty-four years old. I'd never met anyone that was legally blind. That meant, he could see shadows and sometimes his sight would come back, for up to thirty minutes or so.

I enjoyed speaking with him, but I wasn't sure if I could help him. "Well, you know that I can't help you, I'm too young to buy cigars I'm only fifteen." He reached down into the pocket of his plaid robe." As pretty as you are, I am sure Havid will sale cigars to you. I assumed that Havid was the store clerk, so I asked who Havid was and I was right.

The old man ordered me. "Go inside of the house and look on the coffee table to the left. There is a pen and pad on the table. Write a note I will sign it."
I went through the gate and walked up to the porch. There was a strong stench of stale cigar smoke and day old beer. I walked inside of the house there was clutter everywhere. I used my shirt to cover my nose. The condition of his home appeared as a mild case of hoarding. There was trash piled on the tables and in the corners and fruit flies everywhere.

I grabbed the pen and pad off of the coffee table and hurried out of the door. When I walked onto the porch, I uncovered my nose and asked, "What do you want me to write?"

He started thinking, "Okay, say Havid, This is Ant, 'that's short for Anthony you know?' Okay, say this is Ant, please allow my neighbor to purchase my usual case of beer and a box of cigars. Okay, you got that?" I wrote it all down, and gave him the pad assisting him on where to sign.

I verified with him one more time. "Now are you sure that this is going to work? If I waste my time I am going to charge you double." He said to me, "Young lady, I know that it's going to work. I write letters for the Mexican guys all of the time, some of them don't speak English. The funny thing is that I scribble so badly, I don't know how Havid can understand my handwriting." I walked to the store.

Havid was a handsome Middle Eastern guy, very friendly and very serious. I had no problem buying the alcohol and cigars for Anthony. As soon as I handed Havid the note he said, "Oh yeah Ant that's my Partner." But he pronounced it like (POT-NA). "Who are you his niece or something?" "Yeah I am his niece." the note said that I was Anthony's neighbor. Havid didn't even read it. He just heard the name Anthony and gave me anything that I wanted.

I began running errands for Anthony often. He and I developed a beautiful friendship. I even cleaned up for him. In a way, it felt like Anthony was my real family.

By that time I couldn't afford to keep the lights on anymore. I hadn't heard from or seen my mother in a month. Our home phone was disconnected and I had no way of contacting her.

I made a personal space for myself in Anthony's extra bedroom, he didn't mind it, and he enjoyed my company just as much as I loved being there. Anthony would tell me stories of his time in Vietnam. He told me that a bomb blew up in his face and that was how he lost his sight.

"Those gooks were sneaky they fought dirty. Boot camp helped us all become military minded. Ironically the best place to be during the war, was in the war. That is where all of the money was and there was money to be made. There was also lots of sex and lots of drugs. I had a job burning expenditure in fifty gallon barrels and it was easy. I would do my job in the morning and paint the town by the afternoon. I quickly learned my way around town.

The day that we were bombed, I couldn't believe it. A mother with her son, he couldn't have been any older than 4 years old.

He was wearing a backpack I remember thinking that the backpack looked too heavy for him to carry. His mother held his hand walked him into the street then let go of his hand, she seemed to be distracted by something.

The little boy ran away in the other direction and I tried running behind him to catch him. Just like that the backpack that he was wearing exploded. The bomb, blew the kid and everyone around him to pieces. Had I been any closer I would have died.

That was the worst thing my eyes has ever witnessed, a mother bomb her child. When I woke up in the hospital, I realized that I was blind. Ironically, I couldn't grieve. Instead I felt more relieved that I never had to see evil again. Still I don't regret one day of fighting in that war. I gave up my sight for one of the greatest countries in the world and it was worth it."

Anthony loved baking and he taught me how to bake. He would always quote wise sayings like 'a rolling stone gathers no mass' or 'experience makes one wise and wisdom helps one avoid bad experiences.' One of my favorite quotes from him was 'if a man is not dead, he is not a ghost.' For me that quote meant, as long as one is still alive, they had hope.

I called Anthony, Cee-mo (see more). He didn't mind me making up a nickname for him. I knew that he didn't mind, because he would answer me when I called. I thought that nickname was appropriate for him because although Anthony was blind, his wisdom allowed him to see.

I began to spend more time at his house. I was addicted to his wisdom. I practically lived with him. When I was with Cee-mo I didn't feel alone anymore.

One morning, I was heading to the store to run my daily errands for Anthony. By that time, I'd made up my mind to stay with Cee-mo for good. I was even thinking about going back to school.

I was feeling good about myself. On my sixteenth birthday Cee-mo surprised me with a birthday cake. I walked in the door and saw the cake. It was placed on the table, lit with candles. I have never really been the sentimental type, but seeing that cake and that blind man standing there (risking burning his house down) made me cry. It was the first and only time that I had ever had a birthday cake.

I was happy for days but my happiness would be short lived. One day on my way to school,

my mother pulled up on the side of me. "Kandi!"
she was yelling at the top of her lungs, "Where have
you been?"

I responded "Where have you been?"
My mom kept yelling. "What has gotten into you?
Get in the car now, I am shipping your fast butt off
to that place on that Island. I'll let them deal with
you. You ain't nothing but a tramp."

"Hold on mom I am not doing anything!"
My mother was so upset with me. "You haven't
been doing anything? The neighbors told me that
they saw you on East 14Th with a little skirt on.
East 14Th is the blade. I know what those girls be
doing over there. You are gonna catch AIDS if you
haven't already!" At the time I wasn't a
streetwalker, I had gotten paid for sexual favors but
I was too scared to walk the street anymore.

97

I defended myself. "I don't even be over there anymore."

My mom tugged at my arm. She was so upset that she began shoving my head, she was pulling on me and she wouldn't stop yelling. I got into the car I couldn't stop thinking about Cee-mo, I knew that he would be worried about me. My mother was yelling about how I better not be pregnant and it's because of me that she has been running back and forth to court.

While riding in the car she was yelling out asking, why am I trying to ruin her life and blah, blah, blah? In my mind, my mother was the poster child for incompetent parenting. I found it very amusing that she found a way to reassign her parenting negligence as my responsibility. She never came home and she treated me like the bad guy. Cee-mo always said that 'life is like a game of chess.' The sad part in this case, was that my mother used pawns, to checkmate my king.

That's how I ended up in Treasure Island Job Corps, perched over a stack of papers. The agency designed these questions as a way to collect enough information for the counselors to know about me, without getting to know me. That's how things had been my whole life, so I was used to it. I lived in a world with millions of people but no one wanted to know me.

While in Job Corps I was studying to receive my GED. I decided to get a part-time job, because that was a valid excuse for me to leave the campus. I'd gotten a job at a bakery near Union Square. While at work one day I heard a female voice, call my name, "Kandi?" I thought that my eyes were deceiving me, but it was Unique.

My heart dropped into my stomach. I felt the same way one feels on roller coaster rides, when they race down the steep tracks. I screamed with joy and raced over to her. I was so happy "Oh my Goodness Unique! I haven't seen you in hella long. What are you doing here?" She reached into her purse and pulled out her wallet. When she opened her wallet she had at least 3 credit cards. "Shopping" she said. She was so excited to see me. She continued on to ask, "When is your break? Let's have lunch together!" I was ready to go with her anywhere. I wanted her to rescue me from my misery. I instructed her to meet me in the square in 10 minutes.

San Francisco

San Francisco was wild and very eclectic. On the one hand you had 'Old Money' socialites that strolled the blocks of Post St. patronizing Tiffany's, Neiman Marcus, I Magnum and Saks Fifth Avenue. On the other hand there were the grimy, barmy homeless. The city was integrated with cliques of Blacks, Italians, Frenchmen Latinos, Whites, Middle-eastern and Asian. I mean, everyone was there.

Every month there seemed to be marching, Chinese parade, women's rights, gay parade, cancer awareness, and 49er parades. Anytime they could think of a reason to march they would. The city was full of Sassy 'Queens', in-betweens and everyone else. Everyone was together and we were all crazy. The skyscrapers, the ocean views, and the astonishing hills, helped to remind us that we were in one of the most stunning places in the world.

I spotted Unique sitting at a table in the square. She looked like she was a rich tycoon's lad visiting San Francisco on a tour from Dallas. I approached her table. "Hey Girl," I smiled and hugged her.
"Hi Kandi, It's so great to see you. I could spot you from anywhere with that big P.H.A.T horse booty. You're so lucky to have that body."
I flaunted "Yeah I can get any man I want." We laughed. "I'm kidding, I wish." "I see you've finally embrace your body." Unique said, then changed the subject. "I see you have a job, that's good for you." Unique was so happy to see me working, but I was miserable at that job and I finally had someone to vent out my frustrations to.   "Unique, I hate that job. I hate my life. I'm just working because

my sorry ass mother made me join Job Corps. She's
not interested in my future; she just wants to
rendezvous with her fake boyfriend."

After hearing my story, Unique seemed
concerned. "Kandi that sounds hella fake, I'm sorry
to hear that." Unique pulled out a pack of
cigarettes. I didn't expect that she would smoke.
She held out the pack and offered me one. "Try one
it will make you feel better, I only smoke when I am
socializing so what do you want to eat? It's on me!"

Unique was offering to pay for my lunch. I
wondered how easy the credit scam hustle was.
Unique was being so generous.
"Wow! Unique, you look amazing! I wish I could
just get out of that damn job corps." Unique smiled
at me and said, "Girl all that you needed to do was
say a word. I think that I can arrange that for you.

103

My boyfriend knows everything there is to know about computers. He could make you some false release documents." Unique was offering to help and I wanted to hear more. "Yeah girl, give me one of those cigarettes." I reached into the pack that was lying on the table, pulled out the cigarette. I placed the cigarette between my lips and Unique lit it for me. I began to smoke. I blew out the smoke and coughed. I asked, "What do you have in mind?" Unique smiled and threw her cigarette out on the ground. "Put that cigarette out Kandi let's go to eat lunch at Neiman's."

While eating lunch, Unique told me that she'd learned how to perform all type of white-collar crimes, including, check scams, identity theft and credit card fraud. She said that she was dating a blond hair, blue eyed white geek, who loved to smoke weed, have sex and make money. She assured me that she would get me out of Job Corps and from the look in her eyes I believed her.

Unique gave me specific instructions to disappear and not to look back once I got the word. "Kandi, it's going to take up to seventy-two hours, for the Job Corps to verify the information that I send to them. My documents look very authentic. I think that they will let you leave before the paperwork clears. If they let you go, leave and never look back. By the way, did you hear what happened to your old boyfriend Marcus?"

"No Unique, what happened?"
"Marcus got kicked out of that charter school. He got caught in the locker room having sex with one of his class mates."
I was in complete shock. "So where is Marcus going to school now?" I asked.
"Girl I don't know, he is probably running around somewhere out here in San Francisco. You know, he'd fit in perfectly around here."
"I have to get back to work Unique, I hope to hear from you soon."

Unique said. "Oh yeah for sure girl."

A week after seeing Unique I was called into the counselor's office at Job Corps. They said it was an urgent request.

Job Corp could be a scary place at times. It was just as scary for the counselors as it was for troubled teens. My counselor was a dark skinned heavy-set woman who never smiled. She wouldn't even smile when she heard good news. She reminded me a lot of Cherise's mom, except more butch.

I assumed that she was just as miserable as I was. I also wondered if she could fight or was her attitude a mechanism of self-defense. Did she aspire to intimidate people for self- protection? I saw a 'Fem' (Feminine Dike) in Job Corps beat up a butch so bad that she had to get 13 stitches in her forehead. In Job Corps you had to be ready for anything. In the Bay Area it's wise not to judge a book by its cover.

When I went into the counselor's office she told me to pack my things. She said that she received a phone call and documents from my grandmother's lawyer.

"I know that you are doing a great job in here Kandi and you probably don't want to go. Kandi, it appears that your mother didn't have the legal right to sign you up. I called your mother and she denied knowing anything about this matter.

"What matter?" I asked.

"Your grandmother's lawyer sent me the documents that states that she has legal custody of you and she doesn't want you here. We have to let you go. You will be moving to Antioch with your grandmother."
She said to me, "I wish you the best of luck in Antioch, hopefully living with your grandmother will be a positive change for you. You're too smart

107

not to finish school, please make sure that you complete high school at least."

As soon as she said Antioch I knew that Unique was behind this design, my grandmother had been dead for years.

The next day I was given my final paycheck, a Bart ticket and some muni tickets. I left Job Corps without any idea where I was going to go.

Leaving Job Corps was probably one of the worst decisions that I've ever made because when I think back, although I hated Job Corps, at least I was on the right path; I was working and going to school.

Chapter Four

Chapter IV

After running away from Job Corps, I tried calling the number that Unique had given me, but no one answered. I walked around all that day with $120 in my pocket. By nightfall I was exhausted and I still hadn't heard from Unique. I rode the Bart and the Muni all throughout the city to pass time.

I found myself walking around in the Tenderloin district. I saw a sign at a motel that read, weekly rates $115.00. There was a drag queen standing outside smoking a cigarette under the red neon sign. She was chewing her gum so hard; I thought that she would crack her teeth. The Motel was very shabby. I realized that if I didn't get settled in before too late I wouldn't make it to see morning. The neighborhood was worst, than my old neighborhood in East Oakland.

I approached the drag queen and asked, "Can you hook me up with a room?"

She stared at me up and down, continuing to smack her gum. She flung her blond colored wig out of her face and said, "Ooh! Honey you almost got choked. Don't be creeping up on Sugar like that." Sugar was her name; she always referred to herself as a third party.

Sugar had a very pale complexion and always wore her makeup a shade darker to have the appearance of the California tan. Sugar was tall about 6ft., she loved wearing red lipstick and despite her height and her shoe size, she loved wearing high heel pumps. Sugar was sassy, smart, funny and she knew how to beat some makeup.

Sugar helped me from the start, but like I said she was sassy.

111

"Now try asking again, what is it that you need from Sugar?" She said in her rich masculine voice. I was very careful not to offend her, because I needed her. Her demand for respect was intuitive. "Please, I need a room; I'm hella cold out here." I asked as politely as I could.

Sugar threw her cigarette butt on the ground. When she spoke, her vocal tone was slightly deep and she articulated her words in a feminine fashion. "Whew! You lost little girls today! Y'all young ones always need Sugar to help. Learn how to be independent little girl. You mean to tell me that you live in The San-Fran-Cis-co Bay and you ain't got no fake I.D.? Forget it little girl! Where is the money? Dang! I'll do it." She had her own way of scolding me, I liked her immediately.

15 minutes later, Sugar came back with a key and handed it to me,

"Now that is your room, I saw you pay for it. I don't want to come around here in a couple of days and find out that you've let some junkie man come and stay in there with you, you hear me?"

"Okay Sugar!" I replied.

"Okay. Go ahead Lil' girl-"

I now had somewhere to sleep for the week. I was only left with $5 in my pocket. I was so hungry that I thought my stomach was going to cave in. I thought to myself that I needed to get in touch with Unique. I was so tired that I decided to chew some Ice and go to sleep. I would leave my worry and my hunger pains for the next day.

My Dark Alley

I woke up the next morning with money on my mind. I couldn't go back to my old job, Unique told me not to look back. I couldn't go back to Cee-mo. I was afraid that my old neighborhood would be the first place that my mother would look for me. I needed to figure out a way to pay for the room in the weeks to come. I also needed to figure out a way to feed myself...I was starving.

I decided to go to the thrift store and buy a sexy dress with the five dollars that I had left. When I went into the thrift store, I was taken by surprise; all of the dresses were $10 or more. I grabbed a few dresses that I liked and went into the dressing room. I knew a little bit about stealing from watching Fred steal from Mohammad. I rolled up a couple of dresses and stuffed them into my handbag. On the way out of the store, I snagged some earrings off of the counter.

I walked back to my motel room, went inside, sat down on the bed just stared at myself in the wall mirror across the room. I stared for at least 20 minutes. I knew what I had to do. All I could hear was my stomach growling. All that I could vision was my face and my body and that was all that I needed to make money.

I put on the skanky looking tight dress that I had stolen from the thrift store and some shiny clear lip-gloss, and stepped outside of my room door.

As soon as I walked out to the sidewalk a tall thin girl approached me in a vigilant manner. She spoke so softly that I almost missed what she said. She spoke to me in a staid tone. "If you think you're going to work in the 'loin' on my block, without my permission, you are wrong, now get out of here before I cut your throat."

I didn't say anything confrontational, in fact I just looked down at the ground hanging my head and scuttled out of the way. I could hear her voice bellow down the street behind me "And don't bring your punk ass back here bitch." I didn't know where to go, but I knew that it wouldn't be anywhere around her.

The fog was so thick that I could barely see two feet in front of me. The wind blew so strong that despite my hunger pains; my thoughts to relinquish my ambitions were appealing. I walked and walked for at least two hours. I seemed to be walking in circles. My notions of making money this way, was in shambles. In movies, they typecast guys to be dreaming of a girl like me. I was pretty, thick and ready to do whatever.

The only problem was that this was real life. I couldn't find one trick.

116

"Little girl! You better not try to sell yourself to the Po-Po! I know what you're out here doing! Don't look at me like a deer in headlights." Sugar's voice yelling at me from across the street helped me to relieve some tension.
I walked over to her. She was standing in a dark alley. "Hey sugar," I said, "You got an extra cigarette." She reached into her bra and pulled out a pack of cigarettes. She handed me one. "Thanks Sugar."

Sugar was staring at me like a pageant show judge. "Girl where are you from? And why are you in the Tenderloin walking around looking lost?" I thought to myself, they sure like to asked questions in San Francisco. "I'm from The Town. I'm trying to make some money where is all the men at?"

Sugar's head was facing down with her chin pressed into her chest her eyes were looking up at me. "Men? Girl ain't no Men around here gonna pay you. They'll pimp you though! They are just as broke as you.

Watch out for the gangs too. If some of the guys from one of these local gangs see you around here looking lost, they will kidnap you and beat you too. I call them Gorilla pimps and you don't need no Gorilla in your life.

Your best bet is to stay cool, find you some regular clientele, girl get you one of them Mexicans, one of the Mexicans that just got over here; turn some of them into a regular. Follow me girl, let's go into this bar down the street by this time everyone is drunk. This is when they really give up the doe."

We walked into a dark bar. The bar was filled with guys who looked like they could be regulars. They seemed to be in the bar unwinding from a long day of hard work. The bar was very laid back and small. Sugar and I sat down at a table and ordered our drinks from the waitress. Sugar ordered for both of us, two, Long Island Ice Tea's.

As soon as Sugar got a sip of the liquor she began giving me the rundown. "Let me tell you something, this ain't Oakland. City people do things different. You have to learn how to maneuver around BS if you want to survive out here. Now when it comes to Oakland people, they do things with finesse there is a street code. The murder dubs have their code. 11-5 has their code. 6-9 or 8-9 or 9-8 they all have their way of doing things in Oakland. There is a level of mutual respect that hustlers out there have for one another- you don't mess with me and I won't mess with you.

That's how they do it in The Town. It's not like that in the city. These people around here are crazy, Lil' girl. They been on bad drugs all of their life… their daddy didn't hug them long enough as a kid, their boss didn't say hello this morning, whatever the situation is, they are going to use your yellow tail as the weakest link.

In the real world you're a broke black uneducated hoe-bitch. That means when you choose this life, you don't matter; no name, no face! You are the perfect victim.

I don't want to look at the news and find out that your body was found in an alley. Now, do your thing, but be careful. I have to go bend my client over, he just walked up to the bar."

Sugar put her cigarette out in the ashtray and switched away. Sugar was a white man but she reminded me of a wise black woman. "See you girl! Work yo' thing mama!" she said as she switched away.

Sugars advice echoed in my mind as I tried to digest it- 'A broke black uneducated hoe-bitch.' As a little girl, I never knew which career path I wanted to take. But, I surely never wanted to be, who I turned out to be.

My head was a little dizzy, as a result of drinking on an empty stomach. I needed to stand up. I walked over to the bar and asked the bartender for a glass of water.

As I looked around, I thought that the bar must have been in that neighborhood for a long time. The furniture, was worn down red leather stools and chipped wooden tables. Even though the year was 2001, a disco light was hanging over the dance floor like the 1970's.

As I looked around and took a closer look, it seemed as if all of the men were together. I couldn't help but to think that it was my fault for following a drag queen into a bar to look for men. I chuckled a little to myself. The Long Island Ice Tea had really gotten to me.

A young handsome white guy walked over to me and pressed his hand against my back for support.

"Are you okay?" He asked.
I straightened myself up and smiled at him. I cleared my throat and spoke, "Yes I'm am fine, why wouldn't I be okay?"
He smiled back at me. "I thought that you were going to fall, you need to learn how to walk in those shoes better. "I thought to myself- *no he didn't*- I tried to think of something condescending to say back to him. "Don't you have a wife or something~ excuse me, a man to go home to?" He stared at me not offended, not even intimidated, looking directly

into my eyes he said, "Don't you go worrying about what he is doing, he's at home; and stay out of my business?"

The bartender leaned over the bar as he was wiping it down and joined our conversation. "He's my security." The bartender said.
Then the white boy looked at the bartender who was clearly gay, as if they were speaking mental telepathy and said to me out loud, "No I'm not married." With his eyes stayed on the bartender. Then he looked back over at me and said, "And I am not a Fag either."
The bartender laughed and said. "No he is not a fag. He just likes to fuck men up the ass every now and then. Anyway, he is not good enough to be a fag. See me, I'm a Fag, I like to fuck men, suck men, toss their salad -you name it honey, I do it girl."
The bartender pushed a napkin with a few cherries lying on top of it over to me. "Here honey, eat this you just need something on your stomach."

I picked up one of the cherries and ate it. The security guard grabbed a stool and sat down next to me. He ordered a drink for himself. I caught him trying to sneak in glances at me every once in a while.

  Finally, I decided to break the ice. "They let you drink on the job here?" I asked.
He answered me without looking in my direction. "It's club soda." He replied. "What is your name?" he asked. "Kandi, what's yours?"
He took another sip from his drink and told me that his name was Jeremy. We started talking but I wouldn't consider it a conversation. No, not a conversation, just Jeremy asking me a bunch of questions and me answering them. After answering Jeremy's questions, I would ask him the same question, I'd just re-word it.

  I needed to know a most important question though so I asked, "Hey Jeremy- where do the straight guys hang out?" Jeremy looked at me as if he was confused. "I'm a straight guy. I was just joking with you earlier." It was time for me to put my pride aside and be frank with him. "Jeremy, I know you're not stupid. You know why I am here. I need a date. I'm trying to make some money. Jeremy asked with no delay, "How much would you charge to jack me off?"

I couldn't believe it, for some reason he was the last guy, that I thought would want my services; he was so 'pretty. At one point, while talking with him I wondered if he was wearing mascara. "$100" I answered. I didn't know what to say, $100 was what I always charged and it worked with Mohammad...at first.

Jeremy finished his club soda and said "I'll give you $5 to jack me off $10 to titty-fuck you and $15 to cum in your face." I wondered if those were the regular prices for a job like that. "Give me $40 for everything." He looked over at the clock, my shift is over, let me grab my coat. I just live a block from here.

When I walked into Jeremy's home, it didn't look like a man's home at all. There was a huge poster of Madonna over his sofa. The Coffee table was dressed with fancy crystal. He had candles everywhere, with a crystal chandelier hanging from the ceiling. The living room and kitchen were next to one another. The apartment almost felt like the same room, only separated by furniture. There was one closet near the front door. There was also a wall that divided the living room and the kitchen, from the bedroom and the bathroom and there weren't any doors, just an open walkway.

The only questionable 'guy thing' that Jeremy had, was weed paraphernalia. There was a bong on the floor next to a swimming cap and an ashtray filled with doobies.

Jeremy went into the closet near his front door, hung his jacket and removed his shoes. After Jeremy removed his shoes, he put on his robe and slippers. Once Jeremy completed his Mr. Rodgers ritual, he didn't speak very much.

Now he attempted to make me comfortable. Jeremy opened a treasure chest next to his television; that was where he kept his movies. He put a porn movie in the DVD player and walked over to me. He didn't even speak. He pulled my dress down off my shoulders, past my waist and started sucking my breasts.

He was squeezing my nipples and sucking on them. I just remember feeling so grossed out, even though he was cute. He pulled out his penis and pressed it into my chest. I started rubbing it.

Jeremy told me to lie down on my back. When I laid down he straddled over me. He put his pink penis between my breasts, squeezed them together and started pumping and moaning. I assisted him by holding my breast together. I didn't know what else to do. The tip of his penis kept thumping my chin. I needed him to hurry up and get it over with. His orgasm splattered all over my chest and on my chin, I wanted to quickly get cleaned up and get out of there.

I went into the bathroom and I felt so creepy. He had wig heads in his bathroom with masks over the eyes, at least five of them. I washed up and pulled myself together.

When I came out of the bathroom, Jeremy was asleep. He fell asleep on the sofa with his thumb in his mouth. All that I could hear, was moans from the adult film that was still playing on the TV; now watching him sleep.

"Jeremy!" I'm leaving, I need my money." Jeremy opened one eye looking at me he said, "Look over there on the…wait I almost forgot where I was." He jumped up and went into his room. When Jeremy came out of his room he gave me a $20 bill. I objected, "Wait Jeremy, we agreed on you paying me $40." I was upset. He told me to take the $20 and get out of his house. Jeremy began pushing me toward the door. I stopped him. By that time I was tired of fighting loosing battles. "Wait, you don't have to push me, I know how to walk." I opened the door and walked out.

Things weren't working out the way that I planned. I wondered if there was still enough time to get another job. I walked my aching feet, limping to the darkest, most isolated alley that I could find.

My experiences were beginning to make me feel fearless. I saw a car cruising by real slow. I walked out of the alley. Despite my hurting feet, I strutted toward the car in my sexiest walk and asked, "Do you need some directions?" The man stopped the car. I asked, "Are you looking for a date?" He opened the door, I got in. "How much?" He asked "$20 per job" I answered, we pulled around the corner and parked.

The trick unzipped his pants. I asked for my $20 up front. He gave me the money and pushed my head down.

After that job, I made that specific alley my place of business. None of the other girls bothered me there and I didn't bother them. I would give extra change to the homeless and buy them a coffee every now and then. I needed them to be my eyes and ears.

I hung out with Sugar most early evenings and every morning, Sugar visited my room, to make sure that I made it back from the streets safe. Sugar read the daily newspaper, looking for fatalities of other prostitutes. She'd always show me stories, to keep me off of drugs. "You see this Kandi? It's another girl, found dead with a needle in her arm." Besides knowing the daily news, she was in the know about what was happening on the streets. "Do you remember that Lil woman Tracy? Gi-i-i-irl, diagnosed with full blown AIDS. She is on crack so bad, that she sleeps with johns after she runs out of condoms. You make sure, that you put a condom on every penis that you come in contact

with and keep it on. I used to act
nonchalant and say, "Sugar, you are so dramatic."
But I was listening to her warnings.

In those days, I didn't know God. I didn't
know that God had a plan for me. But I know now,
that he was blessing me then and he blessed me just
enough to listen to Sugar.

Usually after hanging out with Sugar, I and
would head back to my alley. I wouldn't say that I
was proud of what I was doing, but I was
independent and I was happy about that. There I
stood, every night in my very own alley waiting on
someone to pay for sex. Waiting on my next trick.

Chapter Five

Chapter V

An entire 3 years had passed since I'd left my alley. I was now a 20year old woman. When I walked away from that dark alley, I walked deeper into the danger zone.

It had been a year since I'd last seen Sugar. Sometimes, I thought of Sugar, but only temporarily. I had a new life now. Michelle was my new name. I learned a few lessons from the streets. I met a few contacts and by now I had a fake I.D and social security card.

I was hard working and careful. I learned how to be elegant from watching drag queens. I planned everything that I did and I mastered the details. I treated each small project like it was important, because I would reach my ultimate goal, by taking one step at a time.

My first assignment, if executed correctly, would gain me tons of respect and lots of money. Betty was my target. The day that I walked into her parlor and she hired me, she was doomed.

Joy or Betty, was a city-slicking teen who'd thought she'd gotten away with running away from her pimp. She had abandoned her former lifestyle and relaxed into the role of business owner. Her eyes told a tale of freedom. Her flat shoes and the way that she walked in them, showed that she was happy to be conservative. However, I did notice her stare at my glamour in awe. My looks, may have played a key role in the reason she hired me so fast. She pointed down at my feet and said, "Wear flat shoes tomorrow," I nodded.

135

I told her, that I would be seeing her later and strolled out of the door in my six-inch stilettos. As I stepped outside of the saloon, the California sun beat down on my face. I slipped my Polarized Prada sunglasses over my eyes and strutted towards the car.

Waiting for me in the car was WoonHa or Lee. All of his friends liked to call him Mack Woon. His American name was Lee. Lee was the name that he used in High School, but by now he was too fancy for that name. The one thing that WoonHa hated was to be called by his American name. Mack Woon had money, power and respect, so he could do whatever he wanted.

After kidnapping me, the first thing that WoonHa did was changed my name. He thought that Kandi wasn't sophisticated enough for his clientele.

I met WoonHa in Reno Nevada. We met under very rickety circumstances. By now, I felt comfortable calling him my Mack and our relationship had made a complete turn.

When I got into the car with him, WoonHa asked, "What happened in there, Michelle?" I looked at him in rage and answered, "I would prefer if you called me Kandi, Lee." I went on to answer him, altering my tone by showing reverence. "It went cool she wants me to start tomorrow." Now this was WoonHa's chance to feel authoritative, Mack Woon snorted some coke off of his wrist and said," Don't mess this up Kandi, we really need this location and I need to use her business license."

He loved to tell me what to do; I think that deep down he felt threatened by my inner strength. "I know Mack Woon, I'm not going to mess up anything." I remember everything that I learned

137

from Cindy about massaging. Then I thought to myself -*Which was all my idea, by the way*-"She didn't even look twice, at my state board papers. She will never know that I showed her a fake license. By now I was irritated by WoonHa. "I have worked hard on this." I ranted. WoonHa nodded at me and smiled. His smile was a strategy to avoid confrontation with the "sassy black girl." I could see that he wasn't in the mood to check me.

WoonHa never spoke very much and he didn't like other people who spoke too much, especially not women. I was the only woman that he'd spare more than two sentences for and that was only to maintain power over me. He believed that when one spoke too often, they would start repeating themselves or lying at some point. I did whatever he said to do, because he changed my life.

The Koreans

Before I met WoonHa, I was desperate and partially depressed. I'd driven out to Reno, to make some extra funds. I lived in Tenderloin. During that time, I was still working my alley. The police cracked down on the working girls in the area so firm, that I couldn't make any money. I had a few regulars and Jeremy who titty fucked me regularly. The only occasion that I could get anything more than $20 from Jeremy, was if he felt like being sodomized by me with his dildo.

I was running out of cash fast. Some local drug dealer started selling laced Tina to the girls. The prostitutes in the area, who liked to take the edge off by getting high, started turning up dead. Narcotics detectives just roamed and roamed the area, asking questions and making business scarce. I left for Nevada.

139

WoonHa was in Reno at the time scratching his itch for gambling; or so I thought. Ironically, WoonHa lived in Sunset, a middle class district in San Francisco.

When I spotted him in the casino, his tailored Tom Ford suit made him a top priority on my 'to do' list. I couldn't help but notice that he kept staring at me, so I tried my luck. When I approached him, I could see that he had the one thing that I wanted and that was money.

I sat down at the end of the bar and he called me to come over to him. When WoonHa spoke, he was very articulate and straight to the point. He told me that he was in Reno for business purposes. He said that he was staying in the penthouse suite. He also told me that he was there to play, have fun and be accompanied by a beautiful woman, such as myself. "My favorite thing to do is spend money."

He smiled at me and said. I just loved men who already knew the rules. I smiled back at him.

I could see that he had money, but I'd been sitting with him for at least five minutes. I noticed that he was drinking but he never even offered me a drink. He looked me directly in the eyes when he spoke and everything that he said was straight to the point. Mack Woon was sexy.

WoonHa gave me his room number and directions to meet him on the top floor at 9pm sharp. Then he winked at me. Although he was sitting, I could see that he was kind of tall, at least 6ft. I expected to turn this fine Asian boy out and get my money, maybe even rob him.

I met up with him on the top floor of the hotel at 9pm sharp. There he was, standing 6ft from the ground; tanned olive skin, mysterious demeanor, waiting for me. To my surprise, he'd changed his clothes into jeans and a white t-shirt. The hip-hop look didn't fit the character that I had fantasized in my mind, but at the time I brushed it off. I just thought that, he was trying to show off his swag for a black girl.

He slipped his card into the door and we walked into his suite. As soon as I sat down, preparing to get into my routine, He asked "Where you from?" just like that. Now he sounded like he was from the hood. I wasn't really there to talk, but I didn't mind helping him unwind.

He reached over and grabbed a small leather box that was sitting on the counter. "You smoke?" WoonHa asked. WoonHa pulled a long blunt out of the leather box and extended his hand toward me. "No" I answered. He looked at me with a confused look on his face, as if he was surprised that I didn't

142

smoke weed.

WoonHa stood up and walked over toward the bar. "I have some Scotch; I'll make yours on the rocks." He poured the drink, walked over to me and set the drink down on the table. I lifted up the glass and took a sip. I looked at WoonHa and said, "I'm only drinking this because I saw you open it and pour it." He smiled, I continued speaking. "I knew that I could make you smile."

His face immediately went back to a blank expression. "What are you doing here?" WoonHa asked me, as if he didn't want me there. I looked at him and answered, "You invited me here."

He looked at me as if he was upset and then he said, "What are you doing here? What is your name?" When he asked the question a second time, I was taking another sip of the scotch that he'd prepared for me. The question confused me and caused me to immediately set the glass down on the table. I figured that he was a little weird; maybe he wanted to role-play.

I chuckled a little because this wasn't like my encounter with Jeremy. Jeremy was a weirdo, I expected him to be rude, but I couldn't figure out what WoonHa's intentions were. I answered his question, with a question. "What is your name?" He reached into the back of his jeans and pulled out a .38 handgun. He pointed his gun at me. My heart dropped down into my stomach, I was terrified and feeling faint. No one had ever pulled a gun on me. I reached into my purse and pulled out my hand knife.

I struggled to keep my eyes open, "You laced my drink?" I asked in a mumble. The first thing he said to me was, "Listen good, if you want to live don't try anything stupid." In that same moment, another guy entered into the room. The last thing that I remembered was hearing WoonHa say, "Never bring a knife to a gunfight." I passed out.

I woke up to grunting and moaning noises. I had been mattressed. I was tied up by my hands and a sheet over my head. I could hear two men speaking in a foreign language I assumed it was Asian origin.

I just laid there in extreme fear, with my hands still tied up. I didn't know whether I should scream or if I should be still. When one guy finished another would climb on top of me. My head was completely covered. I tried to squirm and kick but I got punched in the face so many times that my face felt numb and I was weak. I couldn't even feel the punches any more, I passed out again.

When I woke up I was terrified. The Koreans had removed the pillowcase from over my head my hands were still tied. I could see that I had been moved to another location. I wasn't in the hotel room anymore. My body was sore all over from being raped and beaten.

The handsome Korean man, Mack Woon, was sitting on a chair just staring my naked body. Then he asked, "How old are you? You look like you're only 15 or 16."

"I'm 17 and fuck you, you yin-yang, chop-chop suey eating, Chinese muthafucka!" He smiled and said, "'you're a stupid whore. You think that I am offended by your words? I am not offended by your ignorance, I expect that from you." I wasn't religious but he scared me and I did considered praying.

He was pointing his gun and talking. "You know what does make me offended? I get offended when people get in the way of my money. Every whore that walks in the casino and decides that they have something for sale, needs to ask me first. And you, I wondered what would make a piss colored nigga-hoe-bitch, think that you can just come here, into my territory, open up the cash register, take my money, and walk out? Cause when you came in this casino hoeing that is what you were doing." He held the aim of his gun at me so accurately that I thought I would be dead at any moment.

There was a noise at the door, people entering into the room. It was two beautiful girls, and a man. The girls, a white girl and an Asian girl, just went into the bedroom and starting changing their clothes.

The man with the two girls began saying

147

something in a foreign language and then he said to them in English, "You do what I say."

WoonHa smiled and asked, "What is your name?" I answered this time. "My name is Kandi." For some reason, I still can't figure out why, I felt safer when I saw the beautiful girls. Even though I had a gun pointing at me, I figured, I might have a chance to live if I cooperate.

"Well Kandi you look and smell cheap!" I answered with a question "What are you talking about? You just mattressed me." WoonHa smiled and said "Kandi, who is your nigga?" "My nigga is in East Oakland, waiting for me to come back home." I pretended to have a pimp, hoping that they would let me go. "East Oakland?" Mack Woon said, "I know you ain't that nigga Sean Droop's Hoe! That's the only nigga in east Oakland with a bitch as fine as you."

148

The distinguished Asian sat on the edge of the bed, looked over at his friend and said, "Deuce this chick is lying son and she ain't from East Oakland. I ain't gone lie, I have never had a black girl before, never even considered looking at a black girl, but you are beautiful. Lucky for you, your sex has good reviews.

They say that sex with a black girl, is some of the best sex that a man could ever have. I would have killed you if yours didn't live up to that reputation. I will still kill you, right here and now, if you don't cooperate with me. Things will be fine as long as you do what I say." I remained quiet. "I can see that you choose the latter."

WoonHa looked over at his friend. "Deuce, get her ready and load her up with the rest of the girls." Flashes of light from a camera blurred my vision, as they begin to take pictures of my naked

149

body from the waist down. The man that Mack Woon called Deuce, opened my mouth and forced some sort of drug in a pill form in my mouth. He covered my nose and mouth, until I swallowed. Woon was yelling something in Korean, then he switched back to English, "that's enough, don't kill her son!" I passed out and stayed asleep for what seemed like an eternity.

I awoke in a place that was dark and smelly. I was weak and helpless. I don't remember eating and I don't know when or where, I used the bathroom. The only thing that I knew, was that the room was darker and scarier than my alley in the loin. I was so weak, that I fell back asleep.

One morning, I woke up and I was very clean, as if someone had bathed and dressed me. I was wearing an expensive robe that seemed to be the best that money could buy. The room looked like a King's chamber.

Woon was sitting near the bed just staring at me. "Good morning, Kandi. I have some clothes for you. I want you to get up and get dressed. I have a very important client that wants to meet you. It would be in your best interest, to treat him like VIP."

I was so scared, a sadness blackmailed my spirit. I was broken and I was weak. Voices of laughter echoed from the next room. People were actually laughing, during my mourning. How could life treat me so selfishly? **The cold eyed Korean stared at me and said,** "Your mines now you got that? You gonna make money for me, for the rest of your life. I running this and if you think about going anywhere or trying anything slick, you might as well cut your own throat, because you're dead." I believed him.

Woon presented that proposition almost three years ago, I was 17. At the time I thought that WoonHa and his crew were Chinese. At that time, I thought that every Asian person was Chinese. I later learned that they were Korean. I also learned that Mack Woon and his crew, were some of the most hardcore thugs from the Bay Area. They ran an operation that extended across three states and back to Korea.

WoonHa or Lee was originally from Funk-town a small neighborhood in Oakland, California and that explained why he was simultaneously smart and gangster. That also explained how he had so much power, before his family moved to San Francisco he was friends with some of the hardest thugs in Oakland.

I did everything that Woon told me to do. The Koreans stopped lacing me up, they didn't have to lace me up with dope like they did some of the other girls, because I obeyed. Woon pimped hoes as young as 14.

As long as the hoes needed a crutch they were controllable, so Mack Woon gave them as much drugs as their hearts desired.

I quickly learned that I was gaining favor and trust from Woon. I realized, that when I helped keep the stable organized by mentoring the other girls, Woon spoiled me with more material thing- I made things easier for him. I made sure that the girls showed their loyalty to the family. I even started slapping them around, because it seemed to keep Woon content and it kept him from slapping me. Abusing the girls also made them fearful of me and gave me power.

I was naturally a very organized person; I learned to be organized from my mother. I translated my organizational gifts into a business skill. I slowly found myself in a position of madam (the first lady). Mack Woon placed me in charge of the house and I ran that house with an iron fist.

WoonHa always kept his cool. He was calm and collective, for sure. I developed the biggest crush on him. I wanted to sleep with him so bad and he knew it. Most of the girls had a crush on Woon. Woon always played hard to get, unless he felt he was losing his edge, then he would treat us to dinner.

The young girls did what they were told with no emotion. In the daytime they were shipped off to a parlor and held in dark secret rooms, where men came to drive away at their innocence, via train.

Chapter Six

Chapter VI

I had become mesmerized by Woon. I'd
never known anyone in real life that was so
powerful. When I joined his family I didn't ever
struggle financially. I had corporate clientele. Men
that smelled like the most expensive cologne that
money could buy. I shopped at the most fancy
boutiques and traveled frequently, to fulfill the
needs of clients all over the country.

Drugs were available by the bundle. We
were easily selling and snorting a 1pound per day. I
finally traveled to euphoria, via cocaine. I loved the
drugs, because I felt it gave me energy and
confidence. I fooled myself into believing, that
drugs made me sharper and more competent than
the other ladies.

I had a sharp eye for loopholes and a keen sense of problem solving skills. At the time the operation seemed untouchable. The Koreans would brag to one another saying "uliui sigan jeon-e!" And that is to say we are before our time.

Mack Woon, rented a great condo for me in the financial district. He wanted me to have a private space from the other girls, because he thought that it was smarter for business.

Shopping sprees were the norm. I was spotted around town with Woon often and he splurged on me. "I want all of these nigga's to know that you're mine, I got the finest dark meat on this side of the world." I was the only woman that he trusted, besides his one living female relative, his Aunt Ae Cha.

For our two-year anniversary he took me on a weekend cruise to Catalina Island. During our trip to Catalina Island we had sex. We were facing each other and he told me to turn around. I thought that he wanted me doggy style, but as soon as I turned around he tossed my salad. I could tell without him saying that he wanted me for a long time.

I didn't know what to think. He was making loud breathing noises and then he shoved himself into me. He was slapping me on the backside and sticking his finger in my butt. Beside the one time with Marcus, I would never let anyone go anywhere near my anus.

He was passionate. The sex was wild and animalistic, and we loved it. It was the first and only time that we'd ever had sex. We only spoke about it one time after that and never again. He made it clear that for girls like me sex, wasn't about love or

159

even fun, it was about business.

Woon spent the rest of that trip gambling and laid up in his suite with a cute young blond. He made me work the vacationing Johns, He gave me a goal of $10,000 and told me that if I didn't earn the money before the end of the weekend he was going to beat my ass. I worked for thirty-two hours straight and earned $8,000. Woon gave me a black eye.

After our trip he started spending the night at my house, I told myself that he was in love with me in his own way and he just didn't know how to show it. One night after our trip Woon came over my house and we smoked a blunt together. He'd gotten really comfortable and told me that he had Cindy (one of the older girls and his first girlfriend) since she was 14. He said that he raised her and that she was good at what she did, but she wasn't

160

ambitious.

As Woon sat poised, there in my apartment, he told me his plans. "This business is bigger than you and I. Bitches are going to be selling pussy long after we are dead and gone. It is not enough anymore to have a bottom bitch who don't know shit. Getting money is easy Kandi. In the good old days, a real hoe knew that she had to fuck. These hoes today, they don't see the big picture. They step out of line after making a couple of G's, but what can you buy with 2 racks? After the money is gone up their nose, then they want to run back to daddy.

These bitches need me. The world needs me. Kandi look at me, as long as you trust me you will never worry, these politicians keep creating laws, they say 'let's end prostitution! Let's end pimping and pandering' now they are calling it human trafficking. They got my potna Ramone locked up... The politicians get on TV and speak some fancy speech against the game, but afterwards they

161

pick up the phone and call me, to fuck one of my hoes. That's why I'm raising you right. You can handle the big problems and small problems- but what will you do without me huh? Go to work somewhere for minimum wage $5 or $6 per hr. No you're too fancy for that. If listen to me and trust me, we are going to rule the world...together."

From that day forward, I decided that I would dedicate my all to him, for the rest of my life. I decided that I was going to be his lifetime partner. I fantasized of us dominating an empire, just like he said.

We mapped out a plan together, how the business would run step by step. We followed every graph down to a science. I was the HBIC (Head Bitch in Charge), and everyone knew better not to cross me. WoonHa set up a few of the girls in a loft, in the financial district not far from where I lived.

The other girls worked out of the back of a massage parlor. No one knew where WoonHa or I was living. Things were going fabulous.

Everything changed when WoonHa's cousin Jimmy came to the United States, he chose to live in New Orleans. He said that N.O. was a big city that one could get lost in and that it was close enough to the water to escape if he needed to go on the run.

Jimmy was older than WoonHa and his age difference, caused WoonHa to respect Jimmy's judgment over his own. WoonHa communicated with me less and less and began snorting more and more coke. He seemed stressed, and he acted like I wasn't his partner anymore.

163

After Ramones' 20year sentence, Jimmy came up with the bright idea taking Ramones' job and shipping the girls around.

I told WoonHa that I hated the idea "isn't there a name for that?", "Human Trafficking"; that's what they called it during Ramones trial." Woon look at me directly in the eyes and said very calmly "Shut up bitch!" In my opinion we were doing fine the way things were going. Woon rejected my opinion. I told him that all of the girls were happy. He didn't want to listen. "How do you think you got to the US Kandi? Slavery makes the world go round, it's been that way since the beginning of time."

By the next week we started shipping the girls away one by one, our lives were no longer glamorous. The demand for girls became more rapid. I was recruiting girls more often than I was working tricks; I was kidnapping really.

I hated what I was doing to the girls. I would
stake out their homes or place of business and learn
everything about them. I found a way to befriend
them and once I earned their trust I would lace their
drink. I watched them pass out. Jimmy and the other
guys would then come in and take the girls away. I
realized how important Ramone was to the game
and how his absence changed everything.

The Rest of Betty & Ramones' Story

Ramone operated his business old school style, **he wasn't** a snitch nigga and he was about his money. He really wasn't too sensitive either, that's how I knew he must have been getting high when he made the gorilla move, by throwing that hoe out of the window. We all thought that he would get away with it too, but things had gotten to the point where his freedom jeopardized too many careers.

Our Back up plan if things were to go wrong with Ramone, was to let Jimmy take care of the business in Kansas City. But, there was no way that Jimmy could fill Ramones shoes, I mean the guy spoke four different languages. Woon was making enough money to pay his bills, but he was terribly stressed. His drug addiction had gotten so bad that his appearance was suffering and he'd deserted his decision making skills. He spent a lot of time in the

166

casino and even more time at home sleeping. I was one of the only people who knew where he lived, so I would go over his house every day and make sure that he was eating. He was thinner than I'd ever seen him.

Every now and then Woon would come to his senses, put on a nice outfit and try to dictate the business. The day that I went to Betty's job interview, was one of those days. He insisted on coming with me, to see my new target and hear all about my plans. When he found out that I'd found Betty in San Francisco, that fueled his engine to see her for himself.

After I got into the car with Mack Woon. He drove his Porsche away from Betty's saloon into the traffic. I could see on his face that he was proud of me for having his back.

We stopped by the loft to change cars, then we drove to Van ness to pick up some of the girls from the blade. One of the girls that we nicknamed white trash got in the car complaining, again. "Dang my feet hurt its hella hot out there, I can't be doing all of that standing around in the sun- Police driving back and forth. Tricks was on us though, but I'm finna start working out of hotels, I can't do these cars."

Woon calmly and quickly responded. "Bitch you work where I drop your trifling ass off at. Now give me my money before I make you stroll your way back to the loft."

Every pimp has to think on their toes because their reputation is always on the line. Mack Woon pulled the car over and stopped. Mack Woon looked in the back seat at white trash, reached over the seat to collect his money and said get out my

car. You gone hoe your way back to the loft."
White Trash responded, "But Mack Daddy I'm
sorry, my feet hurt." Mack Woon looked over at
Cindy and commanded, "open the door and let this
trash get out of my car." Cindy opened the door,
stood outside of the car to let white trash out. Now
Cindy was getting upset and demanded. "C'mon
bitch, get out you heard what daddy said."

As white trash exited the car Woon
delegated a new sales goal for her. "I want to see
you at the loft in two hours with five more G's"
Woon put the car in gear and drove away. White
trash stood in the street, staring, with hurting feet
and a look of confusion.

Once we reached the loft, we greeted the
rest of the girls who had already returned. Located
in the financial district, the loft was a large space
with very little furniture. All that was there, was one

love seat and about ten mattresses on the floor. No one who lived in our building, would ever believe that there was a whore house in their building. We were always very quiet and we were very discrete. On the other hand, it was probably the best place that some of the girls ever lived. They were mostly only there to sleep. The loft was an ideal place to live, but the girls, were packed in that place like sardines.

WoonHa still lived in his deceased parent's home, despite the fact that he could afford to live in Russian Hill or Sea Cliff. His home in the Sunset was the home that his parents moved to when he was in high school. In my opinion, it was probably the only place that he felt at ease in. Woon's parents died in a car crash and the house was the only memory he had left of them. His excuse for still living there was that he was trying to stay under the radar; whatever the hell that was supposed to mean. Every time WoonHa would say under the radar, I couldn't help but to think that no person who wears thousand-dollar suits and drove Porsche's was trying to go unnoticed.

WoonHa's one living mentor his Aunt Ae Cha, was the one in charge of the girls at the loft. Most of the girls were young, picked up in various places across the country. The operation was very organized and very lucrative. There were 14 girls in the loft at the time and everyone had a work schedule. Each girl was expected to stick to that schedule or there would be consequences.

WoonHa was very particular meticulous about hygiene. In the beginning he expected every girl to maintain first-rate appearance. We flaunted new manicures. Once a week we would visit the hair salon. For me it was the finest human hair that money could buy, bought in bundles imported from India. Twice a month we'd shop Saks Fifth Avenue.

171

We spent a lot of money on fragrances, cosmetics and shoes.

Some of the girls had corns on their feet as big as knots they would stuff their feet in shoes at least two sizes too small because Ae Cha believed that it looked sexier and more sophisticated for a woman to have small feet. While having sex, they never removed their stilettos.

We always shopped three or four at a time to stay 'under the radar.' That way we looked like a few friends out having a good time. The girls that I traveled with were Marcy, Leila, and Kim. We looked like movie stars. Men would go crazy with lust and women would stare in admiration, sometimes envy. During our daytime shopping trips, we would also network and meet clients to service later that evening.

Ae Cha was confident that none of the girls would run away because she knew that they were more intimidated of her than the police. She would make threats that she would burn them alive if they tried to leave. The runaways who had families looking for them, were afraid that they'd end up in a foster home or Ae Cha would set their families homes on fire. Woon never housed any girls younger than fifteen, he quickly sold them. White trash was Woon's youngest girl at the time.

White trash returned to the loft in two hours and ten minutes with fifteen hundred dollars that she'd just earned to give to Woon. Woon was already gone. If Woon had still been there in the loft he probably would have mattressed her for missing her goal. Ae cha was tough but she wasn't as cruel as Mack Woon. Ae cha whipped White Trash in the shower with an extension cord and sent her to bed with no dinner.

Working with Joy or… Betty

The next couple of weeks I shadowed everything that Joy did. I made it a point to get her few clients comfortable with receiving my services, so that when she disappeared they wouldn't really miss her. I earned her trust very quickly. Betty didn't even investigate my false state board documents.

The day that WoonHa and Jimmy kidnapped Joy, she was in the salon doing inventory and balancing some books. I walked in to her office and politely offered to refresh her tea. She laughed at me and said, *"what you doing Michelle? I have to finish work. I don't know why you being so nice, but go ahead. Just know that you're not get raise."* I smiled and grabbed her cup. That is how I drugged her, I laced her tea.

I watched her take sip after sip. Once she started nodding I said, stand up and don't say a word it's time for you to go. "*What?*" She said, I pulled out my nine and pointed it at her. "*Michelle, is you serious?*" I aimed my gun at the stranger who was addressing me by my alias and replied. "Do I look serious bitch?"

One of Woon's guys Jesse Lee walked into the room and grabbed her. He forced a sock in her mouth and tied her up. Joy tried to kick, scream and fight back, but she was helpless. I held my gun to her head, "There is only one way out." She fainted.

Jimmy, tied Joy in the next room onto one of the massage tables and strapped her legs to the rotating iron leg rests used for Brazilian waxing. She was limply wiggling and wiggling, until I had to help hold her down. Jimmy began beating her to make her stop struggling. Finally, she was strapped in firmly. She passed out again from the drugs and beating.

WoonHa came into the room with three guys. I helped Jesse-lee strip off Joy's underwear, the first guy shoved himself inside of her than the next guy then the next guy. Throughout the day more guys came to have sex with her. It lasted about three days non-stop, sexual violation, I didn't have the feeling of accomplishment that I awaited. I was the lookout for such a heinous act of violence. While I witness Joys punishment flashes of my experience being mattressed invaded my thoughts. No matter how uncomfortable I felt, business had to continue on as usual.

By the fourth day WoonHa looked at me and said she's ready, I have a client for her. Clean her up. Joy was incoherent, they'd doped her up with Roofies because she kept waking up panicking. As I washed her up, she used all of her might to raise up her head she looked at me in the eyes and said *"Why?" She was crying "why? I come here for a better life. You woman, You know it wrong."* She dropped her head and passed out.

A white van came into the back alley to pick her up. I never saw Joy again but while snooping around once I overheard Woon ask about her. Jesse Lee told WoonHa that he'd sold her to a stable in Florida. Jesse-lee went on to say to Woon, "Why you keep asking about that snitch Joy bruh? Your game is getting out of pocket."

That was around the time that things had gotten really ugly. Most of the girls were living in a secret room inside of the parlor. There were no more trips to the salon all hair and nail maintenance was performed there and all of the shopping was done online. White drapes covered the windows and no more of Joys customers were coming to the parlor. The only clients that came into the parlor were johns. The parlor was very discreet almost looking out of business.

Most of the girls had moved out of the loft. The only people that still lived in the loft were Ae Cha, and the underage white girls.

WoonHa was snorting cocaine so bad that he started getting sloppy, he only came around for the money and was less business minded. I started stealing thousands of dollars from him and he didn't even miss it. One day White-trash, who'd turned 16 by that time, came down to the parlor talking loud and high out of her mind off of Meth. She was yelling something about the lights being cut off at the loft and the resident association fee not being paid.

WoonHa beat her right there on the street in front of everyone in broad daylight. I don't care who you are, you don't beat a white woman on the streets…ever. Everyone and they Mama who was out there got on their cell phones and called the police. It seemed like the police were there within seconds. I immediately closed the shop down.

WoonHa ended up going to jail for a week, the D.A. eventually dropped the charges because they couldn't find 'white trash' to testify against him.

When WoonHa got home he kicked her out of the loft. The last I heard, she was somewhere hoeing in east Oakland on International Blvd. I saw an ad that she posted online. She looked terrible. White Trash was so beautiful at one time that she had politicians as clients. The drugs had reduced her to dark alleys.

I knew that it was time for me to break free; I had learned all of the game that I was going to learn from WoonHa. The day that I left he knew that something was wrong. He called me on my cell

179

phone and told me to meet him at sushi restaurant in the sunset. I thought for sure that he would try to kill me. I went anyway. When I walked in he was sitting at a table in the back. Woon looked so good to me; the way that he looked when I first met him.

He said to me, "Kandi, I know that you're planning on leaving me, I don't blame you." I tried to deny that I was leaving, I was scared to death. "Don't lie to me girl, I'm Lee, I'm your Daddy. I raised you." WoonHa went on to speak. "I've messed up big time, We, Jessie Lee, Jimmy and I, kidnapped a girl from Orinda and the feds are on my ass. That bitch is long gone, probably in Nepal somewhere. I gotta get out of here. Kandi, you're still young, you have business sense, go back to school and try to start over. Forget this shit, get out of the game.

I'm going to give you $75,000 that's enough for you to live until you can figure out what you're going to do. The money is in the Louis Vuitton bag under the seat." He got up threw $100 bill on the table, to pay his tab. He kissed me on the forehead and said, "I should have listened to you, you're a bad girl." Woon walked out of the door and out of my life forever.

Tears streamed down my cheeks as I watched the love of my life and my best friend, depart from me. I wanted to follow him, but I knew that whatever trouble he'd gotten himself into must have been terrible, That day with Woon freeing me was like Massa' trying to free a Texas slave and like a Texas slave I loved my oppressor, I thought that I couldn't live without him. His decision to protect me, made me love him that much more.

Chapter Seven

Chapter VII

Along with the seventy-five grand and the money that I'd stashed away, within three years I had obtained $120,000, a Mercedes Benz and about $30,000 worth of jewelry; not to mention, I had tons of clothes, shoes and cosmetics. One of the smartest things that I could have ever done, was keep the location of my residence a secret. I was low-key enough to disappear for a while.

I lounged around my condo, week after week then the weeks turned into months. I realized that I couldn't survive off of $100,000. My monthly rent was $3,500 and that wasn't including utilities.

North Richmond

I began the search for a modest apartment.
Somewhere, that would be significantly cheaper in
price. I found a cute place in Point Richmond near
the San Rafael Bridge. My view was magnificent
and my rent was only $750 per month. My
community was very quiet and very low key. I'd
always been a loner, but I felt myself getting
lonelier by the minute. I considered getting a job,
but I spent so much time smoking weed that I was
paranoid. I was afraid that my past would come
looking for me.

A Local project in North Richmond was only five
minutes away, across the train tracks, so weed and
drugs were extremely accessible. I met my weed
man while shopping at the local mini-mart.

Initially, he was trying to make a pass at me. When

I looked him in the eyes, I could see that he was only flirting, nothing serious. He was a handsome, saggy jeans thug, with enough gold in his mouth to feed an African village. I started to ignore him when he asked if I had a man, but then I realized that he smelled like weed.

I asked him if he knew where I could buy a pound of weed. He looked at me like he saw a ghost. "Damn Baby do you know how much a pound of weed costs?" I answered "No, how much?" He looked up in the air as if he was guessing from the top of his head, I don't think he even knew. "I can get you 1 pound for a 2 G's." I smiled and responded, "Well in that case, I need 3 pounds." The Young man was excited, he offered me a deal. "I can get you that for $4,500. How soon do you need it? "He asked, "Right now," I answered, "how soon can you get it for me?"

At first impression, I stereotyped him as an undereducated, drug dealer by default. In my opinion he was so dumb, that he didn't realize that he had one of the most lucrative businesses in the world, dealing drugs, and he wasn't rich from it.

I didn't care, enough to give him game. I wanted to keep him at a distance and giving him game would only draw him closer; I learned a long time ago from the trannies in "The Loin" that if you wanted to stay alive and out of trouble, stay away from straight black men. The only smart black hustler that I ever trusted was Ramone, and he even got caught up and was in jail, probably for the rest of his life.

The weed man wanted to conduct business, but I needed to go home to get my strap. He stared at me impatiently, "Are you busy? Can you come now? It's just past the freeway across the train tracks," he said. I clutched my purse strap securely on my shoulder and answered him. "Well I have to go get the money, can I meet you somewhere? Is thirty minutes enough time?" I asked, "That's perfect!" He replied, "Here take my number and call me when you're ready." He wrote his number on the corner of a brown paper bag, ripped it off and handed it to me. I folded the torn brown paper once and placed it in the pocket of my purse.

I walked home at a speedily paste. Normally I would wonder toward my home in a whimsical stroll, but today I had business to take care of.

I loved walking around the community, admiring the preserved buildings, mom and pop stores and some of the best plants that nature had to offer.

I entered into my cozy apartment. The beautiful ocean view from the patio, featuring waves wrestling around, clashing against one another, increased the value of the apartment. The tree lined mountain peak that the Victorian sat atop, compensated for the dated kitchen and small bathroom. I took a deep breath and placed my keys on the counter top.

The smell of bergamot evaded my nostrils from the heaps of oils that I hoarded. I was grateful for my new beginning. I knew that my peace could end at any moment. Every time I went shopping, I picked up some jasmine or chamomile or some type of chocolate, it was second nature.

I went into my closet and grabbed the small black carry and range kit from the top shelf. I fastened my waist holster and tucked my piece under my sweatshirt. I sported grey sweats and a hoodie so that men would not gawk over my curves. I closed the top of the carry and range kit and stored it back onto the top shelf of the closet. I kneeled down onto the floor of the closet, where I put in the combination to my safe and removed $4,500. After closing the safe, I picked up the phone, dialed *67 and called the phone number on the ripped brown paper.

The weed man answered and told me where to meet him. I grabbed my car keys from the kitchen drawer, snatched my door key off of the kitchen counter and walked out of the door.

My neighbor just happened to be leaving at the same time as me. She was a pushy, elderly white woman, who intimidated everyone in the neighborhood. She spoke softly but had a dominating spirit. Because of her soft tone, I always managed to flee from her without conversation; my method was to avoid giving her any eye contact. "Hey there dear, excuse me!" She called out to me as I ignored her and hurried toward my garage. If I knew then what I know now, I would have made her my best friend.

I managed to make it free and clear from my nosy neighbor. Once I reached downstairs, I pressed the button on my garage door opener. A Silver 300 S class Mercedes Benz awaited me. It was over a year that I owned this car, but every time I looked at it, I felt like it was my first time seeing it. The car also reminded me of Woon. I remember when he took me to the Dealer and said "Pick any car you like." Still, I relied on his approval before ever thinking about selecting a car. It was also Woon's intelligence, drive, and keen sense of business that earned me this level of good taste. I kept my car parked in the garage, because I didn't want to draw attention to myself.

I drove down toward North Richmond, a little past the Chevron refinery. I was given instructions by the weed man to meet him on 23rd street. I had no business on this side of the train tracks, involving in criminal activity, the street was a police magnet. I was afraid and excited all at the same time. I knew that I didn't need to be smoking weed, I needed to be hustling. I was spending money that I really didn't have to spend. I felt like a trick in a way, but I needed some sort of excitement at this point and I was willing to pay for it.

The weed man was standing in front of an apartment complex when I drove my S Class up, to what had to be, one of the most dangerous hoods in the Bay Area. Apartment after apartment aligned one side of the street, while dozens of small one-story shacks assembled the other side of the street-It was like government research gone wrong. There were nigga's everywhere, not black people...niggas! I definitely stood out.

I saw the weed man signaling me to pull over. I drove up next to him near the curb and he got in to my car. He said "damn girl, what you got a rich white daddy or something? This car looks like a spaceship." "I'm not white!" I said, "I'm just light skinned." Actually now that he'd mentioned it, my mama probably was lying about who my daddy was. "You're kinda cute, what is your name again?" I asked "Oh baby I'm Bang! And, you never asked my name. You don't have to tell me your name though; I know who you are… Ms. Berry. You think I'm cute huh?"

I smiled at him; I liked him deep down, even though he was a real city slicker. "OK Ms. Berry, stay here for a minute this is a cool spot. Do you have the money?" I looked at him like he was joking and answered, "Yes I have the money." He confirmed, "The whole $4,500?" I looked in the back seat and then I looked at him, "Yes Bang!" He grabbed the handle on the car door and opened the

192

door. "OK, I will be right back."

Bang, walked through an iron gate where a group of guys were hanging out. It looked like they could have been shooting dice or something. They took a moment to stop what they were doing and greeted Bang with a fist pounds. Bang continued to walk past the staircase and disappeared past the maze of concrete buildings.

Lots of activity was taking place in such a short period of time. One guy, looked to have a car repair service and a car wash set up directly from the sidewalk. He had two cones placed in the street, so that anyone who drove up, knew that was his territory. I saw a young guy drive up in front of the two cars that the repairman was simultaneously working on and handed the repairman his keys.

193

A woman with a bag of goods was going from person to person selling what she had, she was on the other side of the street. A guy pulled up in a Cadillac on the side of my car with gold jewelry hanging out of the window. "C'mon cutie make your next move, ya best move~ I got gold for sale." I shook my head at him; he needed to make his next move be to the dentist, he only had one tooth in the front.

A few minutes later, Bang came dashing back through the crowd, with a blue backpack on his shoulder. As he moved closer toward the car, I unlocked the doors and watched him walk up to the car. He opened the door and sat down in the car. "OK Ms. Berry!" He said, he opened his hand and showed me the quality of bud. This is the best weed in the world. This "Bomb" right here, will have you on your back! so be careful.

Today is your lucky day. I am only charging you 4G's and I am sure that you can make a $2000.00 profit." I corrected him "Oh no honey I am not going to sale this." He laughed at me and shook his head. "Blood! You gone smoke 3lbs? You gotta be kidding me. Do you live by yourself? Never mind, It's none of my business—just make sure that when you leave here you go and get you one of those life alert wristbands. So, that you can notify the paramedics to come get your ass, when you're passing out. Ha-ha!" I laughed with him.

We made the transaction and he got out of the car, just like that, no drama no disrespect, just an easy transaction. When he got out of the car, he told me to call him whenever I needed him. "You've got my number!" I said yeah and drove away.

The only place that I went was to North Richmond and the mini mart. I knew that no one from San Francisco wouldn't even dare think to step foot in North Richmond. I felt safe there.

When I reached my apartment, I couldn't help but to step back for a moment and be thankful. I realized that I just put myself in a very vulnerable position. What was I just thinking? This loneliness was starting to get the best of me. I couldn't give myself praise for being street-smart; I knew that I'd lasted so long from pure luck.

As I placed a backpack that was full of marijuana on the floor of my apartment, I realized that I couldn't smoke that much weed. What kind of life would I'd be living if I allowed myself to become a lazy weed head whore? This was no way to live. Still I huffed and I puffed, like the big bad wolf and eventually, I blew my straw house down.

It was a Monday morning, 6 o'clock, a loud knock
disturbed my tranquil slumber. I thought that I was
dreaming at first until I heard the knocking a second
time. I yelled out "who is it?" "Hello in there, good
morning it's Mr. Anderson." The voice responded.
Mr. Anderson was my landlord. I wondered why he
was here without notice and what was he doing here
at six in the morning? I replied back through the
door "Oh, Mr. Anderson give me a moment to get
decent." I brushed the leftover buds off of the coffee
table and threw them in the trash. I closed my robe
and fingered my hair into place. Just before I
opened the door I remembered to rub the crud from
around my eyes and mouth. I opened the door.
 "Mr. Anderson, How can I help you?" I knew what
my rights were, I really didn't have to open the door
without a 24-hour notice.

Mr. Anderson was a tall very conservative Yuppie. He seemed so white collar, that he could be intimidating at times. The only way that I knew that Mr. Anderson was down to earth, was because he would occasionally use words like 'Hella' or for instance, when he gave me a tour of the apartment the first time, he said that the view was tight. Oh! And did I mention that Mr. Anderson was born and raised Richmond, CA.

Mr. Anderson looked down at me with a look of disappointment on his face. "Kandi" he said, "I am here because I am afraid I have to serve you with a three day notice." I was in shock "What! What do you mean Mr. Anderson? I paid my rent up for the next two months." I couldn't believe an eviction was why he was here. I'd have to find another place to live. I didn't have anywhere to go so soon.

"The neighbors have been complaining that a funny smell has been coming from your apartment, they are accusing you of using drugs. The neighbors are also complaining that since you have been living here. Suspicious looking thugs have been roaming around in the neighborhood. Two of my tenant's cars were broken into."

I was furious I couldn't believe what I was hearing. I told Mr. Anderson that my neighbors were prejudiced. "They are racist Mr. Anderson! They don't think that a young black woman should enjoy the finer things in life. They want it all for themselves."

Mr. Anderson looked at me as if my response was making him upset, but he never interrupted me, he let me speak. "What does their cars getting broken into have to do with me? Is it because I'm black?"

Mr. Anderson answered, "Listen, I have owned this property for a long time. My last tenants who lived in this very same apartment before you, were a black couple. This place was their home and everyone around here loved them and treated them like family. They would still be here; only they had to move into a larger home because they were expecting their first child."

"I trusted you and I told you that I did not allow drugs in this unit" I spoke over him. "Drugs, I'm not on drugs! How dare they speak that way about me and spread lies?" Mr. Anderson was not convinced nor deceived. He looked at me directly in the eyes and told me straight. "I smell weed in here right now. Your complexion looks horrible and you stink like weed. The only reason why I've come here at this time of the morning is because I am trying to be discrete. I didn't want to put this notice on your door, because the people around here are nosy. My other tenants wanted to call the cops

200

on you. I don't want the cops snooping around my property period. I can't afford to allow you, to make me hot. So you have to go."

I had to respect Mr. Anderson. I told him – "Give me the notice." I reached out for the eviction notice as he placed it in my hands. I said him, "24hrs is too soon, I don't have anywhere to go." Then I smiled and said, "Well, I guess I should have thought about that before 'I made you Hot'." I laughed, and he smiled at me, looking with his baby blue eyes.

"Mr. Anderson where do you get these slang words from?" Mr. Anderson didn't answer. He stood up and reached out to shake my hand. I will rent you a U-hall for Thursday." He said "Oh yeah I almost forgot." Mr. Anderson reached into his pocket and handed me a money order reimbursing me for my two-month's rent and my deposit. "See you later girlie." The tall white man walked out of the door. The only thing that I could think was, I always seem to mess up perfect situations. This time, I only had me to blame.

I sat there in my tiny living room gazing out at the view. Tears streamed down the side of my face. I didn't know where I would go, but I knew that I had to pick myself up and move on.

The early morning skies were as dark as night. It seemed licentious to conduct business at this time of the morning. I didn't know where to begin. I pulled myself together and went in the bathroom to wash away yesterday's grime.

As I stepped into the shower, I couldn't help but to think, about Mr. Anderson's ill-mannered way of speaking to me. I thought to myself -*I can't believe he said that I stink.*- I wondered what he smelled like when he woke up. He probably smelled like bad breath. I started to think if he had spoken to me like that a year ago when I was at the top of my game, he would have been begging to eat me and begging me to stay. Instead now that I am 10lbs fatter, Mr. Anderson is begging me to go; he just kicked me, while I was already down.

I had no idea where I was going to go but I planned on being out of the apartment by the next morning. I started by searching for a temporary place to sleep. I searched through the phone book and found what looked to be a really nice, low-key hotel in concord. I called the number on the advertisement. I felt tense, fearful and very nervous. The hotel receptionist seemed to be really nice over the phone.

I booked myself a three-week stay, just in case I'd found a new home sooner than later or worst case scenario the hotel sucked. I felt good about making that first step. I decided to light up my blunt to celebrate. I even popped a pain pill. I thought, why not go out with a bang. Everyone here, knows I'm doing drug anyway.

It must have been the weed because just as I was thinking I yelled out, everyone here knows that I'm doing drugs anyway. I dragged myself around my apartment turned on the T.V. grabbed the bottle of vodka that I kept stored behind the sofa opened it and turned it up against my lips guzzling a swallow that punished the back of my throat. I drank and drank and the last thing I remembered was trying to get up to use the bathroom. I passed out.

I woke up the next afternoon. My head was hurting. I was unorganized and I had very little time to pack. I went into the bathroom to freshen up. I grabbed my car keys and removed a bud of weed and $5,000 from my stash to pay for my hotel room boxes, some Mexican workers and storage.

I hurried away in yesterday's attire. Finding boxes was a synch. I just needed to organize my schedule and I could be out of Mr. Anderson's hair by midnight. I found a storage space nearby; while the receptionist was filling out my papers I sat in the car and rolled a blunt. It took about forty-five minutes to get business at the storage company taken care of.

All that I needed to do now was pay for my room and find someone to help me move my things into storage. To my surprise when I entered onto the freeway there was bumper-to-bumper traffic. An accident occurred and CHP closed down three lanes. I contemplated on whether I should smoke my blunt or not, but the longer I waited in traffic the better the idea seemed. I began to smoke, the two-hour traffic delay into Concord seemed like an eternity.

I didn't know anyone in Concord. Once I finally reached the hotel, I paid at the front desk I checked in and decided to take a look at my room. The room was nice. It wasn't as luxurious as advertised, but it was good enough to serve its purpose.

The room was furnished with nice mirrors the typical floral drapes, a desk, a microwave, a bed, two nightstands and a dresser. The window displayed a view of the parking lot. I thought to myself, I have been showered by better and bathed by worse. I needed to sit down. I took a deep breath and sat down at the desk. I only needed to go home and pack. Then I thought, forget it, I need some rest. I comforted myself with the thought that I shouldn't be so full of pride; Mr. Anderson has offered to help. I'll make it easier on myself and just accept his help. I'll go home pack my things and wait for him to rent the U-Haul.

Now that I had a legitimate plan and a temporary place to stay I felt a bit relieved. I reached in my purse for my sack of weed and blunt shell and rolled the fattest blunt that I was capable of rolling. I was so stressed that I took a 5-10drag; it's when you inhale for five (5) seconds and exhale for ten (10) seconds. I smoked my weed, turned on the TV, and before I knew it, I was off into a peaceful sleep.

I woke up the next day with a pounding headache. The bright California sunshine beaming down directly into my eyes made me crave a Vicodin pill. I had two Vicodin left in my purse and I was anxious to pop one. As I walked over to the sink for a glass of water I couldn't help but to notice a familiar face flash in front of the television screen. Unique was on the morning news. There was Unique's picture and a splitting image of a fine white boy right before my very eyes.

I rushed to grab the remote and turn up the volume on the television. Unique was in real trouble. She and her boyfriend were facing charges of identity theft, bank fraud, credit card fraud, and bankruptcy fraud. Unique was facing 6 years in prison if convicted. I didn't know what to think, times were different now, we were all grown up but I couldn't help but to remember how kind Unique always was to me. I realized that there must be dozens of people who hated her today but I couldn't help to remember how kind her heart was once upon a time.

I swallowed the Vicodin placed the do not disturb sign on the door and laid down. I fell asleep watching a movie. When I woke up it was 10:30 pm. I contemplated whether I should leave the room but I just figured that there wasn't anything that I could do at this time of the night. I smoked the rest of my weed and went back to sleep.

The next morning I felt much rested I dreaded the fact that I would be facing rush hour traffic. There were cars lined up for miles heading towards San Francisco. This was the kind of thing that made me not ever want to live a "normal life." I was in that traffic for an hour. A drive from

Concord to Richmond would typically take twenty minutes when not facing traffic.

When I finally reached my apartment the garage door opener was not working. I thought to myself that this was a sign that it was time to go; I thought, I need a new battery in this remote. I parked my car on the streets and went up to my apartment. My key wouldn't unlock the door; I double-checked to see if I was using the right key. I'd been smoking tons of weed recently, maybe I was hallucinating. The locks were changed.

I stood there at the door for about a minute just staring at the door I didn't know what to think. I snapped out of my daydream and took a deep breath I took my cell phone out of my purse and dialed Mr. Anderson. Mr. Anderson's phone number had been changed; the new number was not listed. Suddenly everything around me seemed to be

210

spinning in circles.

I decided to go to the neighbor's house to see if they knew what was going on. When my neighbor opened the door she said "oh, there you are I thought that I would never get a chance to meet you, you're always rushing off in a hurry or locked up in that house. How are you dear?"

The little old lady with her wrinkled porcelain skin looked so gentle yet so strong. I could see that she took very good care of herself; she seemed so perfect. Hello, I don't mean to disturb you but have you spoken to Mr. Anderson?" she looked at me like she was confused. "Oh no dear, I think that he is already gone to Switzerland, He and his family left yesterday. If you need anything I'm in charge until the management company finds a new buyer."

I couldn't believe Mr. Anderson didn't tell me that he was moving. And what was this talk about a new buyer. "What do you mean new buyer? Mr. Anderson sold the property?" My neighbor just looked at me and chuckled "Yes she said, I thought that you knew, I thought that was the reason why you were moving. I saw your movers last night they were here all night just banging on the floor and bumping into things. You sure did pick an awkward time to move."

I thought that I was going to faint right there. I'm trying to get inside and get my things. I didn't order any movers." My neighbor backed away from the door and began looking around her apartment. "Oh honey I have the keys to all of the units let me find it, its somewhere in here. Oh! Here it is!" she led the way up to my apartment.

When we got inside the apartment was completely empty. None of my things were inside. There was not a trace or any proof that I'd ever lived there; they even took my mail. "See Honey" She said there were movers here last night with a truck and everything. Or was that the night before? You know I can never remember anything anymore I keep getting my days mixed up." I was quiet for a few seconds and then it was as if I was having a nervous breakdown, I screamed, "WHERE IS MY SHIT!!!"

The other neighbors came rushing out of their apartments. I was screaming and stomping and shaking. My neighbors were so afraid of what I would do. "Calm down! You need to get out of here, I'm calling the police!" I looked at the tall man with the receding hairline and I rushed toward him. I tried to swing at him I wanted to fight anyone. Everything that I'd ever worked for was in that apartment and I didn't have a clue what happened.

The strong bald white guy grabbed me and said "get out of here you are not welcomed." I just wanted my property. I tried to tell him, I begged "Please anyone did you see who it was? What did they look like?" The bald man's wife came up into the apartment, "Hey listen," She said "we don't know anything! Please leave before we call the cops. If someone took your things file a police report there is nothing that we can do."

I wanted to spit on her she seemed so cold so unsympathetic "You know what" I said, "Fuck you Bitch! Fuck you with a sick dick, I hate you! I hate all of you! All of you are prejudice!!! I hate you!!! All of the men grabbed me. They literally picked me up and carried me out to the sidewalk and threw me on the curb. I laid on the street and cried and screamed. Just like that I was homeless and broke.

I got into my car and drove around I just
couldn't think straight. I got tired of driving around
in circles I just wanted to park my car. I found
myself sitting in my parked car outside of Bang, the
weed man's, apartment complex. I sat there for what
must have been three hours. Finally I saw Bang
coming outside. I contemplated whether or not I
should say anything. I blew the horn he looked up
saw me and waved.

Bang walked across the street towards my
car his gold teeth glaring and his pants sagging
down to his ankle. He was tall and fairly handsome
but he had more confidence than Denzel
Washington. He walked up to my car window. I
rolled the window down and told him to get in the
car. Bang sat down in the car and asked me what
was wrong. He said that I looked as if I was crying.
"I was crying," I told him. He told me that whatever
the problem was, it would be okay.

Bang asked me "What are you doing over here? Go home you can't smoke all of your problems away, you're too good for that." I said to him, "I could use some weed right now but I got bigger problems than that. I'm here to conduct some business, but it's not the type of business that we've finalized in the past." I had something else in mind. "Well from the looks of it you're a baller." He said, "I'm willing to hear what you have to say." I looked at him and asked, "What do you know about pimping?" Bang smiled "I know a little why?" I hoped that he didn't think I was speaking of some type of super-fly pimping like in the movies.

"I want to start a stable and I need your help." Bang smiled at me the whole time and said "Well Ms. Berry I have a couple of bitches, I have two hoe bitches that I keep on the track, but I really wasn't trying to make a career out of pimping. I don't like waiting for no one to bring me my money; I'd rather hustle. When I have to wait too

216

long for my money, I'm ready to kill one of them hoes. Is that how you getting your money, by hoeing-up?"

Me, asking Bang for his help was like Oprah asking Jerry Springer how to become the number one talk show host. Bang didn't really seem too interested in starting a stable but he was curious. "Are you trying to be a bottom hoe or something Ms. Berry? You think that pimping can get me a ride like this?" "I know it can Bang!" "Okay Ms. Berry I'll tell you what, I'm down with you, maybe, but what are you going to do for me? You know that if I am your pimp, your loyalty lies with me, right?" "No Bang you have misunderstood what I am trying to tell you. I'm taking about a state of the art operation. I'm talking about girls from all over the world working for you. We could make millions of dollars."

"Like I said Ms. Berry, if I go down, if I end up in prison, I'm not going down for no chick. If you're with me, you're with me. Why you need me anyway? You seem to be doing fine on your own."

"I'm not doing fine Bang I just got double crossed by some shady people, they took advantage of me because they knew that they could get away with it, they caught me slippin' that's all."

I have to start all over again, I need someone on my team, and my instinct tells me that it's you. You have the swag that young chicks will fall for. We can make a lot of money Bang." "Oh okay Ms. Berry, so you want to pimp me, huh? Just like I thought, I'm tryna see what you working with."

Bang was sitting there waiting for me to answer. Bang was a typical Richmond native, he had his own style, he meant what he said and he said what he meant. I had never been with a brother like that, I wanted to raise him and he wanted to raise me. I began to think, I should do it, what could I lose?

"Hey Bang!" I said, "What are you doing tonight?" He answered, "That's what I'm talking about, I'm coming with you baby."

I drove Bang to my hotel room in Concord. He was so impressed. The room was average but Bang thought that the room was so immaculate. As soon as we walked in the door he started pulling on my clothes. "Wait let me get comfortable," I said. "No" he responded, "Take this off!" He was demanding, it was kind of turning me on. I started taking off my shirt, he helped me.

Bang was passionate. He undressed me and Bang kissed me all over my body, passionately. He was generous he was eating me like a 5 course meal. I liked it, something was happening to me, I never experienced an orgasm before, and it was my first time. I was moaning but this time I was being sincere. Usually when I moaned it was to turn a john on, so that they could cum faster.

During my orgasm he was moaning yum, yum, then he whispered "yeah baby that's it cum on daddy's tongue." He kept talking to me, it was driving me crazy.

We stayed in that room for at least three days, laid under each other talking smoking having sex watching movies. I enjoyed Bang and he enjoyed me.

On the third morning together, everything began to change. Bang got up and went in to the bathroom. He turned the water on and I could hear him speaking with someone on his cell phone. I listened carefully and I heard Bang say, "Hey baby, you miss your Daddy? Alright Daddy is going to come see you later tonight." Bang hung up the phone, came out of the bathroom looked at me and said, "Get dressed, 23rd is on tonight! All you gotta do is stroll 'bout one block~ they gone be on you. I'm gone be right there for you okay?" I answered "Okay" "No from now on you say okay Daddy!" Bang demanded. Bang's swift pimp tongue caressed my emotions, as every word cultivated my brain down to it Limbic System. "Baby we not gonna be living in this room for long, we are going to hustle and buy us a house. Yeah, I'm going to buy you a house in Dublin baby. Now get dressed let's go!"

Bang drove me to a street in Richmond flooded with hoes, I would never make money with this much competition. "Daddy I don't know much about Richmond, will these chicks out here try to jump me?"

As Bang sat behind the wheel of my Mercedes, he seemed a little irritated by me. In his Ike Turner tone he said, "Baby how are we going to buy a house and move out of that hotel if you are scared? You can do this baby, now I need you to get out there and get me that money. I'm going to get someone to help you, she knows this area, you gone be cool, trust me."

I got out of the car and stood there chewing the same stick of gum that I'd gotten from the concierge two hours prior at the hotel. It didn't take long for a trick to pull over and request my services. "Damn Bitch, you fine!" He complimented. "You like what you see baby?" I asked. Five minutes later I was $40.00 richer, well that was easy!

222

Four tricks later bang returned with two more girls. Ms. Berry this is Peaches and Layla. Peaches is going to show you around, put you up on game about the area. Did you make some money yet?" "Yeah I made $80." "$80, aww hell naw bitch! How da fuck we supposed get our house and you out here playing. You been out here for at least an hour. Give me the money! When I come back you better have made some fa sho scrilla."

Bang sped away in my car. I stood there in the street nervous and afraid. I had plans to have a talk with him later when we got back to the room, in the mean time I planned on stashing away some money and opening a savings account.

Making money in Richmond was a breeze. I had been working with bang for 4 months by then. There were five hoes in our stable and the tricks were cashing us out by the dozens. Sometime we

223

would get dropped in Oakland uptown or on San Pablo in west Oakland. I still stayed in the hotel out in concord at night but Bang was barely sleeping with me anymore.

I had calluses on the bottom of my feet from walking in stilettos it was very hard for me to save money because Peaches was always there monitoring every dollar that I made. I was tired of hopping in and out of strange men's cars so I wanted to introduce a new way to Bang, a way for me to make money too and be able to get some rest.

One of the few nights that Bang came over to my hotel, we were sitting around watching a boring movie and I asked "Daddy, we should have enough money by now for a down payment on the house, when are we going to start looking?" A side of Bang that I never seen before emerged. He immediately jumped up and slapped me. I tried to jump up and hit him back then he punched me in the eye. I fell to the ground. "You raggedy hoe don't you ever question my money again, you live where I say you live."

Bang was breathing hard and mumbling something, as I lay there holding my eye, "Put your shoes on let's go!" As I put my shoes on, I was silent and he was silently waiting. Then he said, "Hurry up I gotta get back to the Rich! It don't take that long to strap a stiletto!"

Bang was being a jerk and I was curious, why did he make me think that he wanted to buy a house? I was just confused. Maybe he was just stressed out over something.

We left the hotel room and I drove him back to Richmond with the music turned up. When he was getting ready to get out of the car, surprisingly he kissed me on the cheek and whispered in my ear "Damn you taste delicious Ms. Berry. I don't want to see you smoke another blunt. If I see you smoking anything I'm going to beat your ass. I need you to take care of some business, wait for me at the room. You bet not take your ass nowhere go straight back to that room."

Bang got out of the car, slammed the door and walked across the street to greet some guys outside shooting dice. I thought to myself, what have I gotten into? I didn't have any money to rent another room.

After thinking long and hard about it, I'd come to the conclusion that I did want to see him again. I wanted a blunt so bad. He was my weed man and now he's telling me not to smoke weed. I went back to Concord and waited for Bang to show up.

Chapter Eight

Chapter VIII

I was awakened by a knock at the door. I was so excited; I figured that it was Bang knocking. I wanted to see Bang so bad. I couldn't understand why he hit me, he was usually so nice. I thought to myself maybe he was just tired of me, I had gained weight and was constantly complaining about my feet. I was happy that he kept his word and came back to the room, the thought of it made me smile.

When I opened the door, my smile quickly turned into a frown. Bang was standing there, with the cheapest looking hoodrat that I'd ever seen. I left the door opened and walked away, "Who is she?" Bang smiled and said, "You said that you wanted to move into our house right? This is my girl Jewel."

"Your girl?" I questioned.

Bang ignored me and introduced the rat. "J, this is Ms. Berry. She is the one that I was telling you about."

"Ooh uh uh! What happened to her eye? Damn!" inquired Jewel.

This girl Jewel was very loud and scantily clad. Her weave was tired, her lips were black, I assumed from smoking, and she kept scratching her scalp with one finger.

I sarcastically said to bang, "Bang she is not a house, she is a trailer."

"Ms. Berry" Bang said, I need to see you in the bathroom for a minute, we need to talk in private." Bang then looked at Jewel and said, "Bitch sit your ass down, turn on the TV or something; I need go talk to Ms. Berry about grown folks business."

We went into the bathroom and as soon as he closed the door I asked, "What are you doing bringing her here to this room? Why didn't you take her to Peaches? I don't know what to do with her?"

Once again Bang knew exactly what to say to make me comply. "You said that you wanted a house right? I'm trying to help you start a stable of your own, so chill out. Jewel got that mouthpiece; all you need to do is show her how to make that big money, that S-class money that you be making.

When he spoke to me I could just see his lips moving, it was like he was hypnotizing me. I wanted to do anything that bang asked of me.

I interrupted Bang as he was speaking. "Why did you hit me earlier?" He cleared his throat "what?" He said. I repeated myself "Why did you hit me earlier?"

Bang didn't say a word. He stood there looked at me, then turned around, raised the toilet seat and begin urinating and with his back turned to me he said, "You want to have sex and be in love, lay up all day and complain, I want to get money. That is what your problem is. You don't know how to stay focused, keep your mind on business. Ms. Berry, you should know better than anyone, that getting money is our main purpose. I can get money when my bitches ain't staying focused on business. I'm not a hypocrite Ms. Berry. The only thing you need to be concerned with, is thinking of ways to help me get more money. See I'm losing money right now ~ you made me upset, now your eye all swollen up and shit. As a matter of fact, we need to cover that up! Go use some of that make-up, that

MAC stuff and cover that eye up."

Bang flushed the toilet and zipped up his pants. "I want you to take Jewel in there and turn her into you. Get her the best perfume; show her how to get me one of those Benzes, like the one that you gave me. If she gets out of line, I want you to put her back in check." Then, trying to convince me to trust Jewel, Bang spoke softly. "Baby, Jewel is my home girl. She is down to help build your stable. She'll do whatever I say. As for you, you need to do the same, you hear me?" I didn't answer "You hear me I'm serious!" And with a stubborn tone I replied, "I heard you dang!" "Oh and one other thing, you call me Daddy."

We walked out of the bathroom, I don't know what it was, but Bang had complete control over me. When we came out of the bathroom, Jewel was still sitting in the same spot. She'd listened to every command that Bang had given. She was like a stiff mannequin. The scruffy new pimp dimmed the light and commanded Jewel saying, "Take of your clothes." Like a female flee-bag the young girl Jewel followed her master's command.

Bang belted out instruction after instruction, orchestrating what looked to be turning into a strip show. Jewel laid down on the bed at first rolling around and then masturbating.

I had seen a lot of things but this freak show was uncomfortable to watch. "Ms. Berry, I know you're entertained by now, why don't you go over there and kiss Jewel for me. "What" I said "hell no! I don't know where she's been"

"She is clean, do it" I did it one thing lead to another and before I knew it I was engaging in homosexual activity, while Bang sat in the chair watching. When we were done, bang made us take a shower together and go to bed.

The next morning when we woke up Bang was gone. Jewel woke up and started complaining. "Oh hell naw" She said, "This nigga done left me way out here in Concord; I need to go make me some money. I gotta get out of here." I was quick to respond "Shut up! Before I cut your throat. Shut your stupid mouth and wait." I had to say something to let her know that I was in charge.

I caught on fast just like in the city with the Asian girls, Jewel was quiet and laid down on the bed in a fetal position, as she clutched onto her stomach tightly. She moaned and cried, "Oh my goodness, girl I gotta get outta here." I suspected that she was acting like a dope fiend and then I spotted needle markings, "You a junkie?" I asked, "Oh naw this nigga done left me in the room with a

234

junkie."

I thought naively to myself that I was going to end this drug thing today. "Well from now on you're going to kick that dumb habit! we about to get this money. Stand up!" Jewel stood up. I observed her body and from the way things looked she'd been poking herself everywhere. "I can't believe that I didn't see that last night." Jewel said to me in her sassy tone, "It ain't gone change shit."

I was so upset I tried calling Bang with no success "I want you to try to keep calling Bang. You're going to have to kick that dope habit. I am your new mama now we can't make any money if you are constantly getting high. Now eat the rest of that fruit I have over there on the table, you need something on your stomach. I am going to go take a shower and get dressed, keep trying to call Bang."

235

I went into the bathroom and closed the door. I jumped into the shower. I couldn't help but to think that I probably exposed myself to an STD. How stupid of me not to be more careful, I thought. Everything seems to be going so wrong. I felt like I was swimming against a wave, in shark-infested waters. To my surprise things were even worse than I thought. When I came out of the bathroom, I discovered that Jewel had robbed all of my money. My purse was turned over on the bed and she was gone.

I didn't hesitate, I decided to call one of the Koreans customers. I called one of my tricks that I knew through Woon. It was risky but I knew that he wouldn't hesitate to pay me at least $750 and on a good day $2,000. The only thing that I needed to do was to find some really good makeup to cover my eye.

I sat down on the side of the bed and slowly dressed myself. I called Bang on his cell phone He answered, "What's up Baby?" "Hey," I said "I got a trick lined up for later," He quickly attempted to correct me "What the fuck you mean hey? Bitch, you know my name. You address me as Daddy." I wasn't going for it this time "Nigga please! You know that dope fiend bitch Jewel that you hooked me up with stole my shit, now I need some money and I got a business meeting later." Bang raised his voice "What do you mean Jewel stole your money?"

"She said that she was sick, I went into the bathroom to take a shower and when I came out she was gone with my money."

I was so upset I just broke out into tears. "How

could this happen to me I had everything that I needed to do things right this time. I'm leaving the game for good after this I'm going to work this is my last trick and then I'm going to get a job and live a normal."

"Don't cry Ms. Berry. I think you should get out of the game. I remember seeing you looking good, walking around that sadity neighborhood with your latte' in hand. I said to myself back then~ now that is a jazzy woman. I must admit, I was thinking, now that is going to be my woman. I would buy her anything that she wants. I want you to know that money can't buy class. You may be down now, but strong people like us will never stay down. People like us get up and keep fighting. I'm going to help you fight. We can go looking at houses tomorrow. I going to put you up in a nice house maybe we can even start a family just me and you." "What about the other girls?" I asked. "Forget about them let's move away just you and me." Bang answered.

238

I heard a knock at the door. "Hold on Daddy." It's me baby." I opened the door and Bang was standing there looking handsome. He stood there as if he was superman or something. In that moment I felt like he could rescue me. "Ok what ring size do you wear?" Bang asked. And trust me I will deal with Jewel later, right now we need to get you ready for that trick."

We left the hotel room and got into a 1972 drop top Cougar, the tires and rims were so fancy that they cost more than the car. When I got into the car, Bang complimented me, "Girl you're so fine! I can't wait for you to have my baby. Where do you want to go to get the makeup?" He asked me but then he answered his own question. "You know what, I better take you to Macy's." He didn't know better I was used to shopping at SAKS, Neiman's, and Bloomingdales at the least. I'll show him.

"So who is this trick?" Bang was always talking business "He's an old client of mine. How much is he paying $200?" As Bang asked the question I found myself getting offended, I realized that Bang didn't understand the level of business that I was used to. "$200, more like $2,000" Bang thought that I was lying "$2000! How long are you going to be there?" He asked. "10, maybe 15 minutes." Bang sped off to Macy's.

An annoying silence dominated the car ride to the mall. During this quiet space I thought of the danger that I would be in if the Koreans knew that I'd resurfaced. Because not only had I reappeared, I had been conducting business with their clients. I thought that it would be best for me to tell Bang just how dangerous this business was.

"Daddy, I was affiliated with some real dangerous gangsters." Bang touched my thigh and clutched it. "Don't worry about them sucka's, I am affiliated with some real dangerous gangsta's too. Ain't nobody more gangsta than a Richmond nigga. If anybody tries to hurt you, I'm going to kill them. Ms. Berry, you are like a candy, sweet and tasty. You are like a treat to a man, Kandi Treats, that has a ring to it doesn't it?" I knew that Bang wasn't the scary type, but I wasn't sure if he was powerful enough. He had no idea that his association with me could really get him killed.

I kept worrying about what could happen if the Koreans knew what I was up to, they would probably mattress me. Visions of Betty floated around in my head. One bad move and I would end up like her, no doubt. I felt it in my heart that Bang would keep me around as long as I wanted to be there, he probably wouldn't let me go if I wanted to leave. Being with him almost made me feel as if I'd given up on myself, he had my car, he hit me and he set me up with that rat jewel. Out of all of the things that I'd gone through this seemed for some reason, to be the worst.

Divine Intervention

I got what I needed from the mall and Bang dropped me off, back to my room to get dressed.

As the beautiful maroon colored sunset grazed across the evening sky, I strutted across the hotel parking lot. This was going to be it for me. I decided that I would get all that I could from this trick and get out of the game. When I walked into the hotel room, to my surprise, I had been greeted with a .45 handgun and handcuffs. I was being arrested.

"Kandi Trude? You are under arrest for Human Trafficking, pandering and murder. You have the right to remain silent." After the officer told me what I was being arrested for, I began to see everything in slow motion. The room began to spin and I passed out.

I awoke to a stranger flashing a light in my face and asking me the day of the month. "What are these handcuffs for?" I tugged at the cuffs only to experience a tighter grip. "Kandi Trude, You have been arrested. I am Doctor Augustus I am only here to examine you." The doctor turned off the light and looked over at an officer that was standing behind him. "She will be fine." He said.

I looked over at the officer and asked him to explain to me the motive behind such serious charges. I had been a prostitute for years and I was very lucky to never be arrested, but I was no

243

murderer. "I have never even pushed anyone officer. You have got to be kidding me, I am a whore, you can arrest me for that but I am no murderer. As a matter of fact, who did I murder?" I exclaimed. "Ma'am calm down. You are under the arrest for the murder of a well-known Richmond prostitute that went by the name of Jewel. We found her this afternoon, in a hotel parking lot with stab wounds. We have a witness who says that you were with her last."

"What! Jewel? I just met her yesterday. Jewel was a junkie. She stole my money and ran off while I was in the shower. How am I being arrested for her murder? Aren't you supposed to question me first? As a matter of fact don't I have the right to an attorney? I am not saying anything else I need to see my Lawyer. Where is the public defender?" The officer did not speak another word he grabbed me by the arm, stood me up and escorted me out of the medical facility, into a holding tank.

There was the worst set of women that anyone has ever seen in the holding tank There were about twenty girls there, everyone was there waiting to see a judge. The entire room was made of concrete. Two women were stretched out sleeping on a huge concrete brick. The rest of the women were either standing or lying on the concrete floor.

"Kandi?" Someone called out. I hadn't heard anyone call me by my real name since I was a young girl. I couldn't figure out where I had known the familiar face. "It's me Cherise from school. How have you been?" I couldn't believe it. It was Cherise, acting like we were best friends. I spoke to her but I really didn't want to. "Oh hey" I said. She tapped me on the shoulder and said. "Girl, I know that you are not still holding a grudge from elementary school we were babies. Besides, that boy Marcus that we were fighting over is gay now, he isn't thinking about either one of us, trust me." I was shocked. "What? Gay?" I asked. Cherise laughed and replied, "Yes, he is gay he works in Oakland at the county hospital. He decided to study nursing after his mother was diagnosed with cervical cancer. She found out too late and she didn't survive her battle. She was a nice woman."

I had just received an earful in less than two minutes. I sometimes wondered how Marcus was doing. "So Marcus is a nurse now?" I asked. Cherise rolled her eyes and said, "No girl, I didn't say that he was a nurse, he is an x-ray technician. Cherise went on, "He couldn't finish nursing school because it was too expensive. He is doing well though, I saw him last year when I broke my foot trying run from my crazy X." I couldn't believe it, the most perfect girl from school was in jail with me. I felt sorry for her.

"What are you doing here Cherise?" I asked. "Girl, I am in here on old charges I have to turn myself in every weekend to get my driver's license back. This is actually my last weekend, I am waiting to see the judge now then I am going home for good. Girl, I was out there for 10 years, I kept relapsing and committing petty crimes."

"Relapsed? What were you addicted to?" Cherise looked at me as if she was surprised. "Honey, there isn't a drug that I wasn't addicted to."

Cherise surprised me, she had no shame. "Cherise I am not trying to insult you, but what happened to you? You were supposed to be a doctor, honey." Cherise smiled at me and said. "Kandi, I heard a wise man preach a sermon called "Friends?" and in that sermon he preached that only a friend would tell you the truth. You are the first person that has asked me about my misbehavior.

Kandi I was very much loved by my mother and father and very much protected. After being accepted into the charter school, Marcus and I were inseparable, up until the 10Th grade. Marcus was the only person that my parents trusted and would let me go out with. One night, Marcus and I went to a house party together. We were drinking, I only had a couple of sips but I started feeling sick. My vision became blurry and I felt faint; someone had spiked my drink. Marcus led me into a bedroom. There were about four other boys in the room; they all raped me including Marcus.

Marcus kept whispering stupid tease. I was bitter for a long time. I was embarrassed; I didn't want to go back to school. I didn't trust anyone and I couldn't find a reason to live. I started getting high to numb the pain. I never told anyone about that night and now for some reason, I am telling you."

"Cherise Thomas!" An officer walked into the cell and requested that Cherise come with them to go before the judge. Cherise got up "Well that's me, hey Kandi I have been going to this church lately, the church is located over in the village.

I learned that whenever I am in trouble I have a friend that can help me win. I am a work in progress but I am not going to lose this battle. When I saw Marcus in that hospital I didn't feel hate towards him. I was healed because I let go and forgave. I have the lord so I am always going to win. If you call on God you can too." Cherise looked at me in the eye and smiled.

I thought that Cherise was crazy. How could she be speaking to me about God when she was a cracked out dope fiend? I thought to myself yeah right Crack is your only friend Cherise. I thought about it again, in my entire life no one had ever spoken to me about God.

I'd prayed once, at a thanksgiving dinner mom and I attended. One of mom's boyfriends had an aunt that was some sort of a holy roller. But where was God when I was being teased on the playground or when Marcus was molesting me? Where was God when I was homeless and where was God now? The more that I thought about God the more upset I became. I hated Marcus for what he had turned me into. I brushed it off and said under my breath, there is no God. I squatted down onto the hard concrete, then I laid down and fell asleep on the concrete floor; No pillow, no cover, no freedom and no religion.

Chapter Nine

Chapter IX

I served 24 months in the county jail. The murder charges were dropped. The human trafficking and manufacturing charges were reduced to pimping, pandering and drug trafficking. The DA's office scrambled to send me to prison. They tried charging me with murder, then manslaughter, then attempted murder, and finally an accessory after the fact. The charges didn't hold up in court and were dropped.

I was never a drug dealer, but Bang testified saying that I was, to get his sentenced reduced. He told the court that I was Peaches' pimp and his drug supplier. Those charges held up in court.

The public defender wanted me to testify against Bang, but I couldn't live with myself knowing that I had loose lips. The truth was, that I didn't know anything about Bang except that he was the weed man. I know now that Bang was a killer a liar and a snitch.

Turns out, that Bang was outside in his car, on his way back to the hotel when he spotted Jewel leaving the hotel room with my money. Bang and Jewel had gotten into an argument in the parking lot. Bang lost his temper. Bang testified that one thing led to another and Jewel pulled out her knife with intentions to stab him. He says that they tussled over the knife and he accidentally stabbed Jewel to death.

Bang panicked, he didn't know what to do

next so he called the police and set me up. He told the police everything that he knew about me hoping to get a plea deal.

Fortunately for me it was my first offence and I had a very passionate public defender. Despite all of the melancholy that I'd faced in a lifetime, jail seemed to be the worst. Bang was sentenced to twenty years in prison for drug manufacturing, murder and robbery. During the trial they kept using the police code for robbery, which is 211. In the end, I hated myself for trusting that snitch.

While in jail; I'd gotten a job in the laundry room to earn money and to keep myself busy. It seemed that almost every woman in jail was constantly talking about this God character. I couldn't go anywhere without hearing, God this and God that. I wondered if God was so awesome, so amazing, why were they low life criminals? Why didn't "God" give them a better destiny? I also thought about Cherise saying "Friends?"

When I was released, I was so happy to be out of that place. I was free from jail, but I was once again coupled with homelessness. I only had $250 in my pocket. I had no car, no trade and no education; I could barely read.

I got on the bus and rode around Oakland, I was so tired. I got off of the bus in my old neighborhood and just began walking.

Everything looked so different now. For some reason the buildings looked much smaller and the streets a lot more narrow. As I walked, I felt as if I'd stepped twenty years into the future. I was very uncomfortable in such a familiar place.

I stopped in front of a recognizable home. It was Cee-Mo's old house I wondered if he still lived there, if he would remember me.

The time was 8pm, I thought it was a little too late to be visiting someone but I couldn't help myself. I walked up to ring the doorbell.

"Who is it?" A woman's voice answered following an appearance from the porch light. I spoke through the door. "Yes, excuse me miss, I am looking for General Anthony..."

The door opened, a little old lady peeked through the door and spoke behind the black screen gate.

"Oh yes Mr. Anthony, he moved sweetie. He's living over in the retirement home on Fruitvale. Visiting hours are over at 10pm, so if you want to see him, you should probably head that way now. As a matter of fact, I'm headed home now if you need a ride I'm going in that direction."

I didn't have anything else to do so I agreed to accept the ride. Besides, it would be wonderful seeing my old friend, I thought.

As the old lady and I drove a few blocks down to Fruitvale Blvd. she blasted her radio playing that, "God music". I began to get a headache. "Ooh little girl aren't you cold? You're going to get sick out here walking around with that little bitty skirt on." I was still wearing the clothes that I had gotten arrested in, more than two years ago. "I am not cold." I replied, I was freezing.

The old lady dropped me off in front of the home. "God bless you dear." She said. I walked into the retirement home but no one was at the front desk, the old lady told me that Cee-mo would be in apartment E, so I walked over and knocked on the door. "The door is unlocked Ms. Jackson." The sound of his voice made chills flow up my spine. I opened the door. I was never so happy to see anyone in my entire life.

"Hello Cee-mo!" He was older, but I could see by his appearance that he was being well taken care of. His clothes finally matched and he was well groomed.

"Who is that? Is that my girl? Kandi is that you baby girl?" I smiled "Yes Cee-mo it's me." He didn't forget me, he remembered. "Cee-mo, what are you doing in here? You are not that old."

Cee-mo had gone completely blind by now and he was no longer able to live alone. I told him that I always regretted leaving and never contacting him. I told him that I was homeless now and that I was going through very difficult times.

"Kandi reach over there and look in that drawer. My house keys are there, you are welcome to stay at my house as long as you need to. You helped me through one of the roughest times of my life Kandi, you made me want to live again little girl."
"You made me want to live again too Cee-mo. Every man that I have ever known has abused me in some sort of way, even women. You are the only person that I have ever known that isn't a…" I struggled for a moment searching for a word that best described the creeps of my past, "a pervert."

Cee-mo acted as if he didn't hear my testament. He went on to instruct me how to upkeep his home while I was there. "I guess I won't be needing Ms. Jackson's services anymore. I better call her and let her know that you will be living there," said Cee-mo. "She's kind of cute Cee-mo." Cee-mo laughed, "Ms. Jackson can't handle this package that I've got shoot." We both laughed.

Chapter Ten

Chapter X

I'd been living at Cee-mo's house for over month. I visited him in the retirement home often, almost every day. My money was very low. Cee-mo had delegated Ms. Jackson the task of making sure his bills were paid. I didn't have to worry about living expenses, however, I didn't have any pocket money and I was getting restless of living poor.

I tried looking for a job, but no one would hire me, I couldn't find work anywhere. I'd spent most of my mornings searching for work and the rest of my day, I spent hanging out with Ms. Jackson.

Ms. Jackson would come pick me up and drive me over to the local church for free food. I tagged along with her to doctor visits and to check on Cee-mo.

I tried to get Cee-mo to come back home, but he

loved living around all of those old women.

The longer that I waited for jobs to call me back, the more I became stressed and depressed. One day on our way back from getting food, I asked Ms. Jackson to stop over at the local goodwill. I was ready to hit the streets again. I decided that I go back to making money the one way that I knew how and that was by hoeing. I thought to myself that I just needed to be careful. I would buy a cheap used dress and find a corner.

Ms. Jackson was like a kid in a candy store, in that goodwill. It had only taken me about 10 minutes to find a nice dress and some shoes. She was looking through dishes and furniture and bedding, she even bought a couple of bras. "Oh Kandi, you should look around in here for a nice warm coat. You'll need a dress to wear to church too."

I wasn't about to go to church with her- I was going to get my money and move on. I could visit Cee-mo from my fancy new apartment. "What are you going to do with that little dress?" Ms. Jackson asked. "You young girls today don't have any self-respect, you don't leave nothing to the imagination."

I was so fed up with Ms. Jackson and her 'holier than thou' mindset. I'd concluded that I was a pro and I knew what I was doing. My thoughts were that, I administered a million dollar criminal operation before and by trying to stay out of trouble and live a "normal" life, I had been reduced to this beggarly lifestyle.
"You don't know anything old lady, I am tired of you and your imaginary God. If your God is so wonderful why are you still working at 70 years old, standing in line and wearing used clothes? I am sorry old lady, I want more. I don't have time for this right now, just take me home."

I stormed out of the store, out to the car. Ms. Jackson stormed out of the store behind me. "You look here little girl, beauty fades you hear me, beauty fades, waistlines get rounder and your breast began to sag, but the word of the Lord endures forever. I see you prancing around looking at yourself in the mirror. You think that you are something, look at you! You think that you can survive in this world without the Lord. This is an evil corrupt place. You can't turn on the TV without eventually avoiding something demonic TV show. You will not make it without our creator. I don't need fancy clothes or a fancy car to be phenomenal. Look at you, in your prime, you should be graduating from college right now and getting ready to start a family or starting your career. But, you're lost and you can't get a job. You have no work history, no education, you have a jail record and you think that you're going to make it further along in life than me? Well, I have news for you, at the rate you are going you won't get this far. Get in the

265

car let me take you home!"

The ride back to the house was silent- no gospel music, no small talk only silence. Ms. Jackson pulled in front of the house to drop me off. "I know what you're about to do and I am telling you now, it's not worth it. I have grown to love you little girl and I will be praying for you. Mr. Anthony will be going in for surgery on Monday, will you be there? I remained silent and opened the car door. Ms. Jackson continued to speak. "Well I hope to see you there God bless."

I got out of the car and went into the house. I thought about what Ms. Jackson said while I was getting dressed. I couldn't help but to be curious, it was like something was controlling me. I looked over at the bible that laid on the coffee table, I opened it and began to read. "But seek first the kingdom of God and all of his righteousness and all things shall be added unto you." (Matthew 6:33) I placed the bible down on the table and walked out of the door.

I had only walked two blocks and by then a man pulled over in his car, offering to give me a ride. When I got into the car I felt uncomfortable. I kept thinking of the bible quote. I thought to myself I have never given God a chance.

I sat silent in the strange man's car, I took a deep breath and asked, and so what do you like to do for fun?" The strange man touched my thigh and said I like to play with sexy girls like yourself." I looked down at the strange man's hand and said, "You know how this works right?" He reached down on the side of his seat fondling for something. The strange man pulled out his gun and said "No, do you know how this works? Take off your clothes."

There I was, in this car with this strange man and I didn't have any way to escape. "Let me see your hands moving tramp." I was so afraid the only thing I could think to do was jump out of the car. I ran so fast that I ran out of my shoes.

A bullet brushed past my face I ran around a corner into a backyard. I could hear the tires from the strange man's car screeching around the corner. My ear rang from the grazing bullet so loud, that it hurt. I could hear the car circling the block. I hid under a shed I kneeled down and prayed it was my last resort. "Please God, I know that I have doubted you in the past but please lord, show up in my life right now. I need you now Jesus." After about five minutes of waiting under that shed I started off walking home.

I remember praying all the way home and looking over my shoulder. I walked in the door,

268

placed my keys on the table and picked up the bible. I read Isaiah 41:10. "Fear not for I am with you; be not dismayed for I am your God I will strengthen you, I will help you, I will uphold you with my righteous hand.

A peace came over me like never before, I believed God. I'd trusted everyone else, Marcus, Woon, Bang, Myself, but I never attempted to trust God.

I looked over on the nightstand where I kept a pamphlet that Ms., Jackson had given me. She told me that whenever I was ready to open the door for Jesus, all that I needed to say was the words on that pamphlet. So I read it and I meant it. "Lord Jesus come into my life, forgive me for my sins, I believe that you died on the cross and on the third day you were risen again. I make you my Lord and personal Savior." I laid down and went to sleep; it

269

was the most peaceful sleep of my life.

The next Monday Cee-mo died during his surgery. He left me his house and all of the money that he had, which wasn't much but it was enough to hold me until I found a job.

Cee-mo wrote in his will that I was the daughter that he never had and that he was confident that I would find my way. Cee-mo was the father that I never had and the only person from my childhood who truly loved me.

I started working at the same Goodwill that I was always shopping at. I befriended one of the cashiers and she told me that Goodwill was always hiring. They hired me right away. I loved that job I got plenty of training and I loved meeting people and helping customers.

I went back to school. I took a class studying for my GED. After only three months of studying I received my GED test results in the mail, I was now a high school graduate. The thing that shocked me the most, was the small amount of time that it took, for me to accomplish things that I held off for years. I suppose I allowed fear to hold me back.

The goodwill that I worked in thrived because of me. I enjoyed organizing the departments, merchandising the store and helping customers. No one cared what I was doing, so I just took it upon myself to make the most of my workday. I was quickly promoted to manager and I managed my own store. I was good at that job. In fact, I was so good that I was promoted to regional manager after only working there for 2 years.

I now had a successful career and a great personal life. During my spare time, I volunteered at local schools speaking to the kids about sexual abuse and what they should do if anyone was abusing them in any way.

By the grace of God and only the grace of God, I made it out of the streets. I often think about many of the girls, I think about some that I know, who never made it out, how greed, lust and hatred had destroyed so many lives. I think about the chains of fear and how easy it is for a predator to shackle the mind of a loner. I sincerely regretted the pain that I inflicted on others and the role that I played in contributing to the buckets of tears.

It doesn't matter what anyone thinks about my journey, I am Kandi born and raised in Oakland California. The Bay Area made me the streets raised me and God saved me…

KANDITREATS

Child abuse can end today if everyone takes responsibility. Encourage our children, there is greatness in every child. Get help if you are tempted to participate in lewd activity with minors. It is not ok to have sex with a minor. Stop and think about what you are doing if you are tempted to do so and get help.

If you or someone you know is a victim of child neglect, physical, mental or sexual abuse
SAY SOMETHING & GET HELP!

The story of Kandi Treats is fictional. Neither the story nor its characters are real.

Tanisha's Ebonics dictionary

Baller- A rich person

Blade- A street or area where prostitute solicits **sex**

Bomb- High quality marijuana

Boojie- A sophisticated person

Cats- Urban people

Chuch- A Pimp or Mack's Business organization.

Doughnut- A car spinning in whole closed circles. A car stunt.

Finna- getting ready to do something

G- $1000; Gangsta

Game- Street Wisdom

John- A man who pays for sex

Kinda- A little bit

Mattressed- A victim being tied to a bed or drugged, while numerous men take turns raping the victim.

Nigga- A person

Patna- Friend

Pipe- Drugs; in most cases pipe means crack.

PoPo- Police

Potna- Friend

Rack- $1000

Rat - A low class female

Roofies- Rohypol (roh-Hip-nol). Flunitrazepam.
Date rape drug

Scrilla- Money

Shack- A raggedy home

Stable- A home where pimps keep their prostitutes

Stroll- A Street or area where prostitutes solicit sex.

Thick- Curvy toned body; statuesque

Trick- Someone who pays for sex

211- Police code for robbery

5.0- Police

Acknowledgements: Thank you God for everything that you are. May your will be done on earth as it is in Heaven. My Parents Mom, Dad, Thomas Fay, Romander, Diane, Ademola and Curtis. My Nieces and Nephews, My Siblings Lin, Yetti-i-mean, Janie, My Babygirl Ye Wey, Kami, Imesia, Syrita , Chris, Brandon, The Sturghalls. Gwen and Lur. Special thanks to My Big Cuz who woke up every morning during the contruction of this book and let me in your house, only to disturb you by yelling at the computer, Clarence Wilson AKA Clue but I like to call you Clumanati. Aunt Bertha, Thank you Saline Beck. Thanks to the Smith Family, Lagurtha you are a light. My hearts and the apples of my eye, Richard (Midy Widy) Edwards, Ian (Money Waters) Johnson. Kevin (Limp-Leg) Demus, Saritha Puddy C-lo Jones, Manassah (Chocolate Thunder) Handy, Nicole (Nik) Pembrook. Felicia Rein and Howard. Last but not least, Imani and Khristian can't wait to read your books…

Kandi Treats is a fictional story based on the vile reality of the cycle of child neglect and sexual abuse. The story was written to enlighten audiences about the increasing rate of prostitution and human trafficking in the Bay Area. The sexual Solicitation culture can be very complex. I imagined this story based on hear-say.

T-

Dedicated to The Bay

www.ingramcontent.com/pod-product-compliance
Lightning Source LLC
Chambersburg PA
CBHW070324260626
47160CB00003B/940